Yearning for the Holy Land

YOEL RAPPEL

Yearning for the Holy Land

HASIDIC TALES OF ISRAEL

Translated by Shmuel Himmelstein

Adama Books

Illustrations by Irwin Rosenhouse

© 1986 by Adama Books
No part of this publication may by reproduced,
stored in a retrieval system, or transmitted in
any form or by any means, electronic,
mechanical, photocopying, recording or
otherwise (brief quotations used in magazines
or newspaper reviews excepted), without the
prior permission of the publisher.

Library of Congress Catalog Card No. 85–18604
ISBN 0-915361-27-2

Adama Books, 306 West 38th Street,
New York, N.Y. 10018

Printed in Israel

Foreword

The writing of this volume required a great
deal of effort, and I am most pleased to express
my thanks to those individuals who aided me
and those libraries of which I availed myself.
The origins of this volume go back to the time
when I was in Los Angeles, where I was aided
immensely by the library of the University of
Judaism and that of the University of Califor-
nia – Los Angeles (U.C.L.A.). The majority of
the work was completed in New York, during
many hours that I spent in the library of the
Jewish Theological Seminary and the main
branch of the New York Public Library. I
would like to express my deepest thanks to the
librarians who gave so unstintingly of their time
in searching for various sources.

This book could not have been published
without the dedicated work of Rabbi Shmuel
Himelstein, who translated the manuscript
from the original Hebrew and arranged the

stories by topic. My great thanks to him for his aid.

Two individuals aided me throughout. My father, Professor Dr. Dov Rappel, introduced me to Hasidic literature, and guided me whenever there was any question regarding the continuation of the work.

While I was working on the book, I was privileged to meet Professor Eli Wiesel, the noted author. During the course of extensive meetings, he directed me to sources of which I was unaware, made numerous suggestions both on the content and its presentation, and read the English translation. His love of the subject, the breadth of his knowledge and the depth of his insights were a source of inspiration to me, and for all these he has my deepest gratitude.

Yoel Rappel

Table of Contents

Because of Your Son Reuven • Rabbi Nachman of Horodenka – the Rainmaker • Travelling to the Leipzig Fair • Boots for the Trip • All the Way to Hebron • Face to Face • The Coming of the Redeemer • The Maid of Ludmir • A Day a Year • Messengers of Eretz Israel • What Does Eretz Israel Produce? • Maligning Eretz Israel • The Air of Eretz Israel • Eretz Israel Divided Between Them • Rabbi Nachman of Breslau's Trip to Eretz Israel

Introduction

From Longing to Fulfillment

Wherever the Jews went into exile, God's Presence accompanied them. "The exile of God's Divine Presence" and "the exile of Israel" was a basic premise of Hasidic thought about the process of redemption. From its earliest days Hasidism was rooted in a belief in the redemption and the expectation of the coming of the Messiah.

It is told that Rabbi Baruch of Medzhibozh used to mourn night and day for the fact that God's Presence was in exile, and because of his great sorrow never authored any learned works. He explained, "Whoever knows himself as he knows others does not write learned works in this era."

Once Rabbi Baruch was told a new volume entitled *Mayim Kedoshim* had just been printed on the Talmudic tractates dealing with the ritual sacrifices in the Temple. He expressed astonishment at this, and told his listeners, "I find it astounding how a person is able to write a volume on the ritual sacrifices. When I recite the very first paragraph in the *Mishnah* dealing with the topic, it reminds me of the fact that the Temple was destroyed and our own land lies in desolation, and I become dizzy and unable to speak. Here we find a person who was able to write a whole volume on the topic."

In Hasidic thought, God's Divine Presence is perceived as a merciful mother who hovers over and protects her children, the Jews in their bitter exile. It follows that the exile of the Divine Presence preceded the exile of the Jews, as God, as it were, "prepared the way" for His children who were to follow.

The ties between God's Presence and the Jews are strong, and the two are faithful to each other. Rabbi Elimelech of Lizhensk expressed this when he said, "Had we sorrowed only for the suffering of the Divine Presence rather than for our own suffering, we would have been redeemed immediately." We are concerned with our own distress, and God's Divine Presence, which always remains with us, follows us wherever we go.

It is told, Rabbi Elimelech voluntarily went into exile in his youth, together with his brother, Rabbi Zusya. This was a way for them to suffer, and possibly thereby to bring closer the redemption. They wandered about aimlessly year by year, emulating the wandering of the Divine Presence, and they tried to rouse the souls of all they met from their spiritual sleep.

There is only one way that leads to the redemption of the Divine Presence and of the Jewish people, and that is Eretz Israel, "where the imprint of holiness is always strong." But when will this redemption take place?

Rabbi Zusya said, "We find in a verse, 'God told Abraham, Go forth from your land and from your birthplace and from your father's house, to the land which I will show you.' God says to man, 'First you must leave your land – the inner contamination within your body. Afterwards you are to leave your birthplace – the contamination you acquired from your mother. Finally, you are to leave your father's house – the contamination acquired from your father. Only after you have rid yourself of these three can you go to the land which I will show you.'"

The Baal Shem Tov, founder of Hasidism, paved the way, preparing the people's hearts for redemption. A single sentence in a letter he wrote teaches us how much he constantly longed for redemption. On Rosh Hashanah of 1747, the Baal Shem Tov had a vision of the heavenly spheres. In a letter he sent to his brother-in-law, Rabbi Avraham Gershon of Kitov, who was the first of the Hasidim to move to Eretz Israel, he described what he had heard and seen there, and what he had said. Among others, he told of a conversation he

17

had with the Messiah. "When will you come?" he asked him. "The sign of this will be when your teachings have spread and you become known to the world, and when what I taught you and you understand will go out abroad, so that the others too will be able to invoke the Name as you, so that all the hampering impurities will fall away and it will be a time of favor and salvation."

The appearance of the Messiah, who symbolizes the ultimate redemption, is thus dependent on the spreading of Hasidic teaching throughout the world. But these teachings are not spiritually complete and do not have a great deal of influence unless they first pass through the sanctified air of Eretz Israel. Eretz Israel, to which Hasidism always turned, was defined by Rabbi Nachman of Breslau as "simply this country of Eretz Israel, with all its houses and apartments." In other words it is not something outerworldly or something which cannot be felt with one's senses, but the land in the simple sense of the word, and it is that country which must serve as the center from which Hasidism must spread its teachings and ways to the Diaspora, and thereby bring the ultimate redemption closer.

The first one to attempt implement his "demand" for the Messiah to come was the Baal Shem Tov himself, by trying to move to Eretz Israel. He was prevented by heaven from doing so, however, as he writes in a letter to his brother-in-law, "God knows that I do not despair of the chance of travelling to Eretz Israel, if it is the will of God."

There is a legend: When the Baal Shem Tov was once in the heavenly spheres, it was proposed to him that he stay there, and in that way he would not need to feel the pain of dying. He answered, "What can I do? I desire to be buried in Eretz Israel, for it is from there that the souls ascend."

In Hasidic literature, almost all of the greatest leaders are reputed to have decided to move to Eretz Israel and to have prepared themselves for the journey. Many of them in fact even left their homes and began the trip, but "heaven prevented it." The fact that this story is repeated so often about so many leaders characterizes the general spirit and the atmosphere prevalent in the Hasidic movement, which could not visualize the image of a great rabbi, who embodies all the greatest virtues, who did not desire with all his heart to move to Eretz Israel.

They tell: Rabbi Haim of Krasny, one of the greatest of the Baal Shem Tov's disciples, tried all his life to move to Eretz Israel, but was unable to do so. It is told that once he even embarked on a ship which was sailing to Eretz Israel, but on the way a storm arose and the ship sank. Only by a miracle was he saved.

Heaven had prevented him from reaching his destination. The Hasidim explained how this caused him so much grief and sorrow that he did not recover for the rest of his life. Before he died, he commanded that his gravestone should carry no titles, as he had failed in his efforts to reach Eretz Israel.

They tell: Rabbi Pinhas of Koretz, the friend and student of the Baal Shem Tov, also wished to move to Eretz Israel, and even left Ostraha, his last place of residence, in order to travel to Eretz Israel. Legend tells how the rabbi of his town, Rabbi Yiva of Ostraha, exclaimed, "Rabbi Pinhas is a great scholar and wishes to observe the Talmudic saying that if there are two sages in the same time, one will die and the other will go into exile. He wishes to be the one that will be exiled, but I have my doubts if his legs will lead him to the Holy Land." On his way, Rabbi Pinhas reached the town of Shpitovka, where he became sick and died.

These stories, including the ones that are legends, were a product of the atmosphere in the Hasidic movement. More than bearing witness to the move of individuals to Eretz Israel, they are evidence of the great love of the land by the members of the movement and the vivid imagination which wove legends about the actions of its leaders.

Miracles are among the basics of Hasidism. It is thus natural for Hasidism to glorify moving to

Eretz Israel, which is an integral part of its nature, with many stories of miracles and supernatural events.

In the summer of 1764, a few years after the death of the Baal Shem Tov, a large group of his disciples and students moved to Eretz Israel. This group, which was led by Rabbi Nachman of Horadno and Rabbi Menahem Mendel of Primishlan, took sail from Istanbul to Eretz Israel. Many miracles occurred on the trip. There was a great storm and the ship was about to sink. Rabbi Nachman then lifted a *Torah* scroll and proclaimed in front of all the passengers: "If, Heaven forbid, the Heavenly Court has decreed that we die, we the Court on earth, together with the Holy One, blessed be He, do not accept the verdict, and may it be Your desire to annul the verdict."

Rabbi Nachman then ordered everyone to recite Psalms with great devotion until the storm abated and the passengers arrived safely in Acre.

Rabbi Nachman of Breslau's trip to Eretz Israel was filled with miracles. He left for Eretz Israel in 1798 and arrived on the day before Rosh Hashanah in 1799.

When Rabbi Nachman got on the ship, which carried "men, women and children, both of *Ashkenazic* and of *Sefardic* extraction" to Eretz Israel, "there was a great storm, so that none was able to remain alive. All cried out to

God, and one particular night was like Yom Kippur eve (because of the many prayers said), with all crying, confessing and requesting atonement for their souls" (prior to death). Rabbi Nachman then got up and proclaimed, "If you quiet down, the sea will also quiet down. They all accepted his advice and calmed down, and they were saved."

They tell: Rabbi Yerahmiel of Koznitz always thought of Eretz Israel. He used to say, "The Torah forbids jealousy, and, thank God, I envy no person, except for those Jews who travel to Eretz Israel."

In different studies of Hasidism, a number of opinions have been formulated as to the relationship of the movement to Eretz Israel, a relationship which is strongly allied to the idea of the coming of the Messiah and the ultimate redemption. Simon Dubnow stressed the change which occurred in Hasidism. At first the vision was one of the redemption of the nation to one which dealt with the redemption of the individual. According to this view, the move by Hasidim to Eretz Israel had one major goal, the setting up of a Hasidic center in Eretz Israel. The historian Benzion Dinur and the philosopher Martin Buber stressed the Messianic principle in Hasidic ideology. The spreading of Hasidism, especially in Eretz Israel, is a condition for the beginning of the redemption. Gershom Scholem, who researched *Kabbalah*, rejected any vision of Hasidism as a Messianic movement, and, if anything, saw a certain lessening of Messianic fervor in Hasidic ideology.

Together with the question of what links Hasidism had to Eretz Israel, there is also the question of what motivated the Hasidim to move to the country. Scholars have pointed out three major reasons: the desire to set up a Hasidic center in Eretz Israel; the disagreement between the Hasidim and *Mitnagdim*, which became much more intense in the second half of the 18th century; and the worsening conditions in Poland brought about by its dismemberment.

The first Hasidim who arrived in Eretz Israel believed that now their Torah study would achieve its desired completeness, and that the sanctity of the country would envelop their studies. Rabbi Israel of Polachek, who was one of the leaders of the three hundred Hasidim who arrived in Eretz Israel in 1777, describes their first encounter with the country with great enthusiasm and amazement. "This is the day that we have hoped for; let us rejoice in our precious land, precious to all our hearts, joy of all the holy thoughts with all forms of holiness, filled with a large variety of fruits and other pleasures of man, and where all the commandments are performed at the highest level." In their innocence, the Hasidim believed that there was a Divine mystery in their travelling to Eretz Israel, and they regarded each event that occurred to them as a sign from heaven.

They tell: There was a custom in Belz, when water was being drawn for baking the *matzot* (unleavened bread) for Passover, each person would wish all the others, "Next year in Jerusalem." Rabbi Shalom heard this and asked, "Why 'next year in Jerusalem?' We should rather say, 'tomorrow in Jerusalem'. Our redemption can come in the twinkling of an eye, and why should we delay our hopes even for a few days?"

They tell: Rabbi Levi Yitzhak of Berditchev instituted the following custom during the writing of *T'naim* (an engagement party which included a written commitment of the two sides to marry at a later date). They would write as follows: "The marriage will take place, please God, at the following time, in Jerusalem, the holy city. If, heaven forbid, the Messiah has not come by that date, the wedding will take place in Berditchev."

The connection between the Diaspora and redemption, between the profane and the holy, was apparent in the voyage of Rabbi Nachman of Breslau to Eretz Israel. He made the journey when he was 27 years old, a relatively young man, especially in comparison to the age of the vast majority of those who made the trip in order to die there and be buried in the holy soil. When he made the journey, he had no intention of doing so for his own benefit, but rather for the good of his students and disciples. He felt that by being in Eretz Israel he would be able to be infused with the holiness of the land and its Torah, in order to return home and impart some of what he had gained to his followers.

Unlike other Hasidic leaders who came to Eretz Israel in order to free themselves from the impurities of the Diaspora, his trip was meant to bring back some of the holiness of Eretz Israel to the completely profane Diaspora, so that those who lived in exile could taste a little of the redemption. "My place," he said when he returned, "is only in Eretz Israel." Wherever he travelled and every place he visited he always saw before himself Eretz Israel. "Wherever I travel, my destination is always Eretz Israel." All the Torah he had studied before making his trip and all the ideas that he had formulated before that time he regarded as unfit, and he commanded that none of these be written down.

After returning Rabbi Nachman saw Eretz Israel as all-encompassing. The air of Eretz Israel is filled with the Divine Inspiration of God. It is the major source for all thought; it is the true spiritual center of the world. There are Eretz Israel minds and Diaspora minds, but the latter receive all their inspiration from those in

Eretz Israel, for the main source of all wisdom is Eretz Israel. Each Jew has a part in Eretz Israel, and each person in the Diaspora draws his inspiration from the part that he has in Eretz Israel, so that every single person's inspiration traces back to the land.

The sanctity of Eretz Israel exists to this day. God's Divine Presence has not budged from the country, and therefore, according to Rabbi Nachman, "Whoever truly wishes to be a Jew should travel to Eretz Israel, and even if there are many obstacles he should overcome them all and travel there." Israel's redemption can only come about in the place that God's Divine Presence has already been redeemed – in Eretz Israel. The "exile of the Divine Presence" and the "exile of Israel" will only come to an end when all the Jews live in the Holy Land, Eretz Israel.

* * * * * *

This collection of Hasidic tales encompasses a period of about the first 150 years of the Hasidic movement, with the material gathered primarily from sources written between the beginning of the 18th to the middle of the 19th centuries. I chose these stories and extracts from a number of sources, some from original writings, others from various collections; the reader can see the wide range of sources used reflected in the bibliography at the end of the volume.

In phrasing the stories as they are brought here, I was faced with the choice of either quoting them verbatim as they appear in the original sources, or of translating them into modern-day idiom. I chose a compromise, whereby I tried to remain as faithful as possible to the source while at the same time rendering the story more intelligible to the modern-day reader. In addition, some of the stories were only to be found in latter-day collections, possibly because they had been handed down orally throughout the generations.

For the convenience of the reader, I added titles to all the stories in the book. On the whole, these titles are based on the content and underlying idea behind each story.

The Pain of Exile

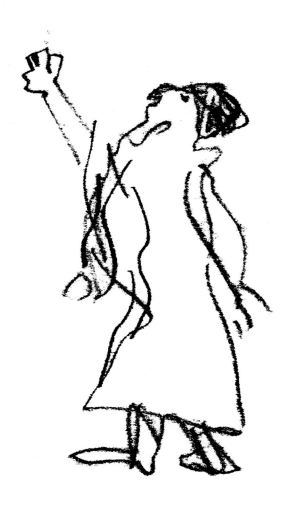

Mourning for Jerusalem

On the evening before Tisha B'Av, the annual fast day commemorating the destruction of both Temples in Jerusalem, Rabbi Avraham, known as the *Malach* (the Angel), came to the synagogue to pray. As the cantor started the very first word of the book of Lamentations, *"Eichah"*, Rabbi Avraham screamed out in a loud voice, *"Eichah,"* and immediately placed his head between his knees and remained silent. There he sat for the full twenty-four hours of the fast, convulsed in grief, as he thought about the destruction of Jerusalem.

Rabbi Baruch of Medzibozh Mourns

All his life, Rabbi Baruch of Medzibozh mourned for the Divine Presence which had gone into exile with the exile of the Jews from their land. Because of his misery, he was unable to compose any books.

Once he was told that a new work had appeared entitled *Mayim Kedoshim*, which was a commentary on the entire *Seder Kodashim*, the section of the Talmud dealing with the Temple service. He immediately commented, "I am astounded how anyone could write a volume on the entire *Seder Kodashim*. When I merely recite the chapter of *Aizeh Mekoman*, which is a small section of the entire *Seder Kodashim*, and I think of how our Temple was destroyed and our land laid waste, I become dizzy and cannot continue to say the rest of the words. And yet here I find a person who has actually written a commentary on the entire *Seder Kodashim!*"

Sabbath is No Time for Mourning

Once Rabbi Baruch of Medzibozh hosted a certain prominent Jew from *Eretz Israel* for the Sabbath. This man was among those who constantly mourn for Zion and Jerusalem, and who are unable to forget their pain over the destruction for even an instant.

On Friday evening, as Rabbi Baruch was singing one of the traditional Sabbath songs and recited the verse, "The lovers of God await the rebuilding of Ariel" (a poetic synonym for Jerusalem), he looked up at his guest, and saw him deep in gloom, as every other day. Rabbi Baruch stopped singing for an instant, and then, turning to his guest, continued the concluding words of the verse in a voice filled with joy, "On the Sabbath day rejoice and be glad as if you had just received Nachliel, the Holy Land."

The Baal Shem Tov Mourns

It is told that every midnight the Baal Shem Tov would rise from his bed to mourn the destruction of Jerusalem, and that there would always be a burning fire surrounding him. Rabbi David of Kalmoye, at whose home the Baal Shem Tov stayed, woke up at midnight, and seeing the fire, picked up a bucket of water to put it out. When he drew near, though, he saw the Baal Shem Tov sitting on the floor and mourning the destruction.

His Correct Address

I am from *Eretz Israel*, but due to our sins we were exiled from the Holy Land, and I am therefore temporarily a resident of Ostrowiec.

Whenever a person is asked where he is from, he should reply, "I am from *Eretz Israel*, but am at present living temporarily in exile."

Awaiting the Messiah

The Messiah isn't Here Yet

Once an insane man went to the top of the Mount of Olives and blew a *shofar* (ram's horn). Immediately a rumor began flying throughout *Eretz Israel* that the Messiah had come. When Rabbi Mendel of Vitebsk heard the rumor, he went over to the window, peered outside, and exclaimed bitterly: "He has not come yet. I see no differences in the world outside."

Discarding the Prayer Book

Each year Rabbi Avraham of Chechanov would buy a new copy of the *Kinot* (Lamentations) prayer book recited on Tisha B'av, the day both Jewish Temples were destroyed. Immediately after Tisha B'av, Rabbi Avraham would discard that year's volume in the pile of worn-out religious objects kept in the synagogue for collective burial. He explained his actions simply: "I am sure that within the coming year the Messiah will come, and next year there will no longer be any need to recite the lamentations."

The Messianic Era

In 1848 the world was in ferment, and rumors circulated that the Messianic era had arrived, that the redemption would soon follow, and that the Rizhyner Rabbi was the Messiah.

When the Rizhyner heard of the rumors, he commented, "This generation does not deserve a miraculous redemption. The Jews will only be freed physically if they are granted permission, without miracles, to return to *Eretz Israel*. What we need to do first is to establish facts rather than rely on our dreams and desires. The beginning of the redemption will be by natural means, as in the days of Ezra the Scribe at the time of the Second Temple. Only after that stage will the true redemption, that of the spirit, arrive."

The Coming of the Messiah

It is told that throughout his life Rabbi Menahem Mendel of Vitebsk kept his ears attuned for the blowing of the *shofar* (ram's horn), the sign that the Messiah had arrived. He explained that this way he would be able to know exactly where he would have to go.

He always extolled *Eretz Israel*, and even went so far as to state that "*Eretz Israel* is the *Shechina* (the Divine Presence) itself." He also used to say, "Even if I am involved in a most complex Talmudic question, and even if there is a serious decision I have to render, I will drop what I am doing and go out to meet the Messiah. Each and every day I expect him to redeem us, and I do not wish to miss even an instant of the times of the Messiah."

Waiting for the Messiah

Rabbi Moshe Teitelbaum eagerly awaited the Messiah all his life. Whenever he heard any type of commotion in the village, he would ask: "Is that the Messenger of Redemption?"

In order to be ready at any time for the Messiah's coming, he would carefully lay out his Sabbath clothing near his bed. A guard was posted outside his room, so that at the first signs of the coming of the Redeemer, Rabbi Moshe would be awakened.

Once, in order to save him the walk, his disciples offered to buy him a home near the synagogue. "But what will I do with it?" he answered. "Soon the Messiah will be here, and I will be moving to Jerusalem."

Another time his son came to visit, and when the servant saw him coming from afar, called out, "He has come." Immediately Rabbi Moshe exclaimed, in the language many use before performing a commandment, "I am hereby prepared and ready to welcome the king, Messiah." When he was told it was his son who had arrived, he appeared depressed.

Each year, on the day before Passover, he would tie a box of *matzot* (unleavened bread) and a bottle of wine to his bed, so that he would always be ready to leave at a moment's notice when the Messiah arrived.

Once, before the *Kol Nidrei* prayer on the eve of Yom Kippur, he looked upward and said, "Lord of the entire universe! Had Moshe, son of Chanah, known that he would grow old without the Messiah coming, he would not have been able to survive for even an instant. But You pushed him off from day to day, and the poor man believed you. Pay me, an old and simple man such as I, for my faith, and send us the righteous Messiah. I do not seek it for my sake, but for Yours, so that Your name will be sanctified in the world, and the world will be sanctified through Your name."

Longing for Eretz Israel

Differences of Approach

Rabbi Menahem Mendel of Kotzk used to say, "I want the Messiah to come, and Rabbi Shlomo of Lantashna wants the Messiah. I want *Eretz Israel* and he wants *Eretz Israel*. I know that we have not yet repented completely, and he knows it. Nevertheless our service of God is not identical and my way is not his. He cries to God to send the Messiah who will bring all the Jews to *Eretz Israel*, and I cry to the Jews to repent before God, so that the Messiah will automatically come and we will all enter *Eretz Israel*."

A Real Achievement

Once the Rabbi of Apta sat meditating, and his disciples noticed that he seemed to be somewhat distressed. When they asked him if anything was bothering him, the Rabbi replied, "In my entire life I feel I have accomplished nothing."

At that instant a messenger arrived from *Eretz Israel*, carrying a letter from the Wahlin Kollel (a higher rabbinic institute) in Tiberias, telling him that he had been appointed to be head of the Kollel. Immediately the rabbi ordered that a festive meal be prepared. After the meal, he gave the messenger a sum of money, and instructed him to buy a burial plot for him near the grave of the prophet Hosea.

On the night that the rabbi died, banging was

heard on the windows of the Wahlin Kollel in Tiberias, and a voice called, "Go out to escort the Rabbi of Apta to his grave." When the doorman went outside, he saw a coffin moving through the sky, surrounded by thousands of souls. The doorman followed the procession, and saw how the body was buried.

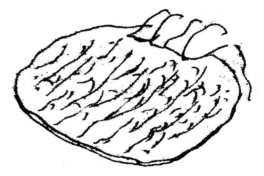

This Year in Jerusalem

The disciples of Rabbi Shalom of Belz drew the water needed to bake *matzot*, the unleavened bread eaten during Passover. By Jewish law, this water must be left overnight before use to assure that it is at room temperature before it is mixed with the flour. Once they turned to Rabbi Shalom and wished him, "Next year in Jerusalem." Immediately their master answered, "Why next year? We may be able to use this water drawn today to bake *matzot* tomorrow, the day before Passover, in Jerusalem, and eat those *matzot* in the company of the Messiah."

Jerusalem And Berditchev

When Rabbi Levi Yitzhak of Berditchev's grandson was to be married, a preliminary contract, the *t'naim*, was signed between the two sides. In that document, Rabbi Levi Yitzhak specified that "the wedding will take place, please God, in the Holy City, Jerusalem. If, heaven forbid, the Messiah has not yet arrived, the wedding will be held in Berditchev."

Drawing Closer to Eretz Israel

Rabbi Aryeh Leib Segal, a disciple of the Maggid of Mezritch, always longed to move to *Eretz Israel*. Whenever he set out on any journey, he used to say that this trip was meant to bring him closer to *Eretz Israel*. Each letter that he sent included the phrase, "on my way to the Holy Land, to life and peace."

Rabbi Aryeh Leib finally was able to realize his dream, and settled in *Eretz Israel*. There he spent his time studying Torah. He was an extremely humble person, and ordered that his tombstone contain only the words, "He loved Torah."

Longing for Eretz Israel

Once Rabbi Nahman of Breslau sat speaking with two of his children's fathers-in-law, Rabbi Aryeh of Valutshisk and Rabbi Avraham Dov of Chmelnik, about *Eretz Israel*, its holiness and its beauty. In the midst of their conversation, the Rabbi of Valutshisk exclaimed: "For the past forty years I have longed for *Eretz Israel*, desiring so very strongly to bask in its glory, and yet I have not been privileged to go there and see it." The Rabbi of Chmelnik was astounded at this comment. "Why should anyone pine for it so long? All one has to do is take one's money and travel there."

Rabbi Nahman came out to his disciples and told them, "The rabbi of Valutshisk will eventually move to *Eretz Israel*, while the rabbi of Chmelnik will never see the country. Longing and pining are more important than all the world's treasures, for the latter decide nothing." A short time later Rabbi Nahman's words were fulfilled.

Longing to Move to Eretz Israel

A number of times Rabbi Yaakov Yosef, the most important disciple of the Baal Shem Tov, attempted to move to *Eretz Israel*, but was told by his master not to do so. The Baal Shem Tov told him, "I will explain something to you. Whenever you wish to travel to *Eretz Israel*, it is a clear indication to you that the fate of Jerusalem is being debated on High, and Satan is specifically bothering you so that you do not pray for the city. This means that whenever you feel you wish to travel to *Eretz Israel*, pray instead for the city."

The Baal Shem Tov's Desire to Move to Eretz Israel

The clearest indication of the Baal Shem Tov's desire to move to *Eretz Israel* is to be found in a letter he sent his brother-in-law, Rabbi Gershon of Kitov, who had moved there. "The Lord knows that I have not given up moving to *Eretz Israel*. If God wishes it, we will be together, but the time is not ripe for this."

His brother-in-law answered, "What can I do, for I know your nature, and you need to pray with your own *minyan* (prayer quorum). Because of this, in addition to other factors, I am afraid that you will not come to *Eretz Israel* until the Messiah arrives."

Eretz Israel And Other Lands

Ascending to Eretz Israel

A certain Jew once came to Rabbi Yehezkel of Shenyava and asked for his blessing. It seemed that he had become bankrupt and was forced to run away to *Eretz Israel*. Rabbi Yehezkel arose from his chair, and with a shout declared, "What do you mean you went bankrupt and are running away to *Eretz Israel*? One runs away to America. One ascends to *Eretz Israel*!"

How to Have One's Prayers Answered

Rabbi Pinhas of Koretz understood the secrets of proper prayer. He used to say that anyone who wishes his prayers to be answered should have *Eretz Israel* in mind as he prays. He should think of the entire country, its borders, its cities, villages and hills. Whoever does so will surely have his prayers answered.

How about those who already live in *Eretz Israel*? What should they think of in their prayers? They should think of all the Jews still living in exile, and beg God to soon return His children to their own home.

What Are We Worth?

Rabbi Shimon of Sheptivka moved to *Eretz Israel* and settled in Tiberias. He used to take long walks among the hills outside the town at the hottest time of the day. Once, as he walked, he realized he had forgotten his snuff box and glasses at home. Right then he saw a young boy approaching, and asked him to go to his home and bring them to him. The young boy refused outright. "Do you know who I am?" the Rabbi asked him. "Of course. You are the Rabbi of Sheptivka." "And yet you refuse to go for my glasses?" Immediately the young boy turned to the surrounding hills and told him, "Right here Rabbi Akiva and his 24,000 students – every single one of whom was greater than you – are buried."

Rabbi Shimshon broke out in tears and exclaimed, "You are absolutely right! What value are rabbis of other countries here in *Eretz Israel*?"

The Duty to Live in Eretz Israel

In his book *Nesi'a Shel Simcha*, Rabbi Simha of Zalozhtsy writes:

"I am absolutely astonished at those who fear God and yet spend all their lives outside *Eretz Israel*, to eventually be buried in those impure lands. I am not surprised at those who place their material wants over their spiritual needs, for to them one country is like any other, and every other country is to them *Eretz Israel*. But I cannot understand the Hasidim, who consider their spiritual needs as supreme and their bodily wants as secondary, and yet live elsewhere. Even if these people spend all

of their lives performing all the commandments and praying properly, they will not accomplish as much as they will within a single year of living in *Eretz Israel*. One cannot compare a servant who works within the king's palace to one who works for the king in an isolated island far away from Him, even though God rules supreme everywhere in the world."

The Land of "Megurei Aviv"

Rabbi Shneur Zalman of Ladi, the founder of the Lubavich movement, gave an interesting interpretation of the verse, "Jacob dwelled in the land of *megurei aviv*" (Genesis 37:1). The word *megurei* has three possible interpretations: it can mean either a dwelling place, or fear, or a feeling of being a stranger.

From the time the Jews were exiled from *Eretz Israel*, the various countries they have lived in have served as a dwelling place for them. It is nevertheless obvious to everyone that these are not secure places, but all have a certain element of danger and fear for Jews. In every other country the Jew feels that he or she is not part of the "mainstream," but is a stranger to some extent. There is only one place in the world, *Eretz Israel*, where the Jew does not feel like a stranger or in fear, and it is only there that a Jew can really feel at home.

Aphorisms

Whoever loves *Eretz Israel* is loved by it.

Each person must beg that God will make him or her long for *Eretz Israel*.

True longing for *Eretz Israel*, a longing which comes from the depths of one's heart, brings about God's mercy and His desire to hasten the redemption.

Eretz Israel unites all of the Jewish people.

Zion is the heart of the universe, from which all blessings emanate.

One who gathers money for the poor of *Eretz Israel* is spared the tortures of the grave.

If one supports the poor of *Eretz Israel*, blessings from *Eretz Israel* flow to the other countries.

The further a place is from *Eretz Israel*, the less the unity in that place.

The Jew has no need whatsoever to find him- or herself a place outside *Eretz Israel*.

In *Eretz Israel* one comprehends the Torah in its *Eretz Israel* garb.

Eretz Israel is the essence of holiness.

Eretz Israel is more holy than the synagogues of all the other countries.

Eretz Israel only belongs to the Jewish people if they speak the Holy Tongue, Hebrew.

Even the most simple person can understand the sanctity of *Eretz Israel*.

The primary source of understanding and wisdom is in E*retz Israel*. Even if Jews are elsewhere, they derive their understanding and wisdom from *Eretz Israel*.

Whoever wishes to be a true Jew – which means ascending from one rung of holiness to another – can only do so through the sanctity of *Eretz Israel*.

It is impossible to move to *Eretz Israel* without suffering, and the greatest source of suffering is those talebearers who spread bad tidings about the country.

Eretz Israel is the major segment and the sustenance of the world.

Eretz Israel is the interior of the world, all the other countries are the exterior.

Eretz Israel is the soul of the world, and is subdued by the soul of man.

Whoever has not tasted living in *Eretz Israel* cannot appreciate the impurity of living outside it.

A person who lives in *Eretz Israel* has the power of influencing those who live outside it.

There are souls which must have only *Eretz Israel* and there are souls which must specifically have other countries.

Rabbi Nachman of Breslau on Eretz Israel

Prayers are more acceptable when offered in *Eretz Israel*.

All holiness comes by way of *Eretz Israel*. Only there is it possible to ascend to the highest levels on the ladder of holiness.

By studying Torah, one may merit the opportunity to visit *Eretz Israel*.

A person who remains in *Eretz Israel* in spite of all the obstacles is a true hero.

Those who donate money to *Eretz Israel* are embraced by its very atmosphere.

By fervent prayer one gains the ability to go to *Eretz Israel*.

It is in *Eretz Israel* that we will see the downfall of the wicked.

In *Eretz Israel* the good will see that what befalls the wicked is what the wicked had wished to befall the good.

Those who move to *Eretz Israel* to attain a greater level of holiness will achieve their aim, while those who go for other reasons will not benefit from the move.

The holiness of *Eretz Israel* aids one to attain faith and patience; it also strengthens one's resolution to forsake anger, melancholy and sadness.

One should always pray to yearn for *Eretz Israel*, so that one will merit the attainment of one's desire to go there.

In *Eretz Israel* one can convince oneself that God provides for everyone.

Eretz Israel is the nerve center of the Jewish people. Each Jew has a share in it, as long as he or she honors God. If one desecrates God's name, he or she loses that association with *Eretz Israel*.

The brain center of *Eretz Israel* works for calmness and peace. Through gifts to *Eretz Israel*, these qualities are absorbed by brain centers elsewhere. When the donors are careless of the honor of God and permit blemishes to appear, they taint the brain center of *Eretz Israel* and cause quarrels there as well. This is the cause of the present-day controversies in *Eretz Israel* and in other lands.

The settlement of *Eretz Israel* best demonstrates God's loving care of the world.

The desire to move to *Eretz Israel* draws affluence in its wake. One who desires to sustain the multitudes draws blessings from Zion to other countries.

Stories

A Story of Eretz Israel

When Rabbi Nahman of Breslau was in Lemberg, he announced that he wished to tell a story, and that it would be about *Eretz Israel*. As the people of Lemberg loved Rabbi Nahman's stories, all came to hear him. He began speaking with great fervor about the country itself, but before he even reached the gist of the story he fainted. All began shouting, and he came to. He exclaimed, "What is all the tumult about? I was in *Eretz Israel* and wanted to bring you there with me, and what a pity that you weren't able to come."

The Redeemed Will Return to Zion in Joy

Once a visitor arrived in Koznitz just before the Passover *seder* meal, and the Maggid of Koznitz invited him to his *seder*. The guest had been drafted by the Russian army while still in his early teens, and his speech was a garbled mixture of Yiddish and Russian.

At the end of the *seder*, the guest requested permission to sing the traditional verses of *chasal siddur Pesach*, in which the Jew thanks God that the *seder* was observed in accordance with the law, and which ends with the hope of "Next year in Jerusalem." Of course the Maggid permitted the guest to do so, and as he reached the last verse, *peduyim lezion berinah* ("the redeemed ones will return to Zion in joy"), he substituted the Russian word *padyom*, which made the phrase read, "Let us go to Zion in joy."

As the guest sang, he edged toward the door. The Maggid, hearing the words, put on his shoes, took his staff in his hand, and in great joy exclaimed, "We – I and all of my Jewish brothers – are ready to return to Zion!" The Maggid and his guest left the house dancing arm in arm, singing "the redeemed ones will return to Zion in joy." As the guest left the house, he disappeared, and all that they heard was the melody fading away in the distance.

I Have Answered You Because of Your Son Reuven

Rabbi Moshe of Savran would not permit his Hasidim to move to *Eretz Israel* unless they were rich enough to be able to live there comfortably. He explained, "I do not want to increase the number of those who speak evil of the land." Whenever a rich man was moving to *Eretz Israel*, Rabbi Moshe would make him a big feast in his home, and greatly honor him.

When Rabbi Yeruham Fishel, who was extremely wealthy, asked permission to move to *Eretz Israel*, Rabbi Moshe immediately granted permission and made a feast for him. Rabbi Yerucham Fishel had no children, and Rabbi Moshe offered a blessing that by the merit of living in *Eretz Israel*, he should be blessed with children.

Among the people at the feast was a Rabbi Rafael, who was extremely poor. When he saw that Rabbi Yeruham Fishel was moving to *Eretz Israel*, he also wished to move, but he knew that Rabbi Moshe only granted permission to the rich. What did he do? He had a friend who was very wealthy, and he went and borrowed the finest clothing from that friend. He then took a fancy pipe and went to the rabbi, hoping he would not be recognized. He too requested permission to move to *Eretz Israel* and it was granted. The rabbi made a farewell feast for him as well. After the meal, Rabbi Rafael asked Rabbi Moshe to give him a letter certifying that he was poor and should be among those eligible for grants from the *Eretz Israel* charity fund. He also begged forgiveness for having deceived the rabbi and not having told the truth. Rabbi Moshe answered him, "Fool! I knew everything that was going on. I nevertheless went through with the entire procedure, but not for you. Everything I did was for your son."

Rabbi Yeruham Fishel settled in Safed, and soon afterwards Rabbi Rafael also moved there. Rabbi Moshe's blessing to Rabbi Yeruham Fishel was soon fulfilled, and his wife bore him a son. He was named Binyamin, after Rabbi Yeruham Fishel's father.

When the child grew, he was sent to the local *heder* (religious school). One day he did not return home from his classes. His parents, in great distress, went looking for him and asked everyone whether they had seen him, but no one had any ideas of where the child was. Finally, they came to the rabbi of Safed, Rabbi Shmuel Heller, to ask his advice as to how to proceed. The rabbi asked them, "Who is his best friend?" When they told him, he called that child and asked him where his friend was. At first the child didn't want to say anything, and kept repeating he knew nothing. Finally he admitted that both had been standing by a pit and had had a competition as to who could jump across it. Binyamin had jumped across a number of times successfully, but the other child had failed in his attempts. Finally, in frustration, the other child had pushed Binyamin into the pit.

Everyone ran to the pit, calling Binyamin's name, but there was no answer. Reuven, son of Rabbi Rafael, was standing on the roof of his parents' house and saw the commotion at the pit. He asked aloud, "What happened?" They told him that Binyamin had fallen into the pit. That day Reuven's mother had set up a clothesline to dry her wash. Reuven speedily cut down the line and ran with it to the pit. He saw that everyone was at a loss as to what to do, so he jumped into the pit. Soon he called out that someone should lower the rope to him. They lowered the rope and dragged him up, carrying Binyamin in his arms, but the child appeared to be dead. They brought the "dead" child to Rabbi Shmuel's house, but he eventually opened his eyes and asked, "Where is the old man?" They asked him, "Which old man?" He answered, "During the entire time I was in the pit, an old Jew held me in his arms, and he saved me." Rabbi Yeruham Fishel exclaimed, "That was Rabbi Moshe of Savran; may he protect us."

Rabbi Nahman of Horodenka – the Rainmaker

Rabbi Nahman of Horodenka was one of the Hasidim who moved to *Eretz Israel* in 1764. At that time, most of the Jews in *Eretz Israel* were of Sefardic (Middle Eastern or North African) origin, and had no idea of the greatness of Rabbi Nahman, who was an Ashkenazic (German or Polish) Jew. They were only able to judge from his behavior that he was a righteous man.

One year there was a total drought, with absolutely no rain in Tiberias. The prayers of the Jews of Tiberias went unanswered. When Rabbi Nahman became aware of the situation, he ordered the members of his community to go to the Cave of Rabbi Hiye, the great Talmudic sage, which was near Tiberias, where they would pray for rain. Even though it was a bright, sunny day, without a cloud in the sky, Rabbi Nahman ordered his followers to bring along rain clothes against a rainstorm. The non-Jewish mayor of the city, who was at the city gate and who saw what was happening, laughed aloud and spat at them. He also threatened that if they would return without rain, he would crush their leader, Rabbi Nahman.

When the Jews arrived at the cave they began praying with devotion, and in a short time the skies became overcast and heavy rains fell on the town. Had the Jews not had their rain clothes, they would not have been able to return home. When they came to the gate, the mayor was waiting for them. He bodily lifted Rabbi Nahman and carried him into the town.

That day, there was joy in Tiberias because of the rain, and God's name was sanctified among all.

Travelling to the Leipzig Fair

Rabbi Nahman of Breslau told the following story to his disciples:

When Rabbi Menahem Mendel moved to *Eretz Israel*, one of his Hasidim, a very successful businessman who was very strongly attached to the rabbi, abandoned all of his business deals and moved along with the rabbi to the Holy Land.

When the Hasidim in *Eretz Israel* realized there was a need to send someone to collect money from the Hasidim outside the country to support their group, he was the natural choice. On his trip, though, the man became very sick and died. Those who lived in *Eretz Israel* knew nothing of his death, nor did he realize himself he had died. Instead, he thought he was on his way to the Leipzig Fair. During the trip, he spoke at length to the personal servant who always accompanied him, and to the coachman, whom he had never seen before.

As they were travelling to the fair, an intense longing overcame him to be with his rabbi, to the extent that he decided to drop what he was doing and leave immediately for *Eretz Israel*. When he told his plans to his two escorts, they were adamantly opposed. Why leave an excellent business deal at this time for such a frivolous cause? When he insisted on carrying out his plans, they revealed to him that he had died, and that they were both harmful angels who had been put in charge of him. He immediately demanded that they appear before the Heavenly Court for judgement, and they could not refuse his demand. The Heavenly Court ruled that he was correct: they were to bring him to Rabbi Menahem Mendel in Tiberias.

When he arrived in Tiberias and entered Rabbi Menahem Mendel's home, one of the angels reverted to his normal appearance and entered the home with him. At first, the rabbi was terrified by the sight of the angel, but afterwards he ordered the angel to remain behind until the rabbi had completed his mission. For a week the rabbi worked on his disciple's soul, until he had perfected it.

Boots for the Trip
Rabbi Tzvi of Kaminka was one of the greatest students of the Baal Shem Tov. All his life he wanted to move to *Eretz Israel*, but since he was desperately poor, he simply couldn't afford the trip.

At that time, there were two fairs in Kaminka each year, one before the Sukkot holiday and the other before Passover. Just before the Passover fair, a poor Jew knocked on Rabbi Tzvi's door and asked his wife for a small favor. He was going to the fair, but his boots were made of felt, so he couldn't do a lot of walking in them. He wanted a place to leave them. He would pick up the boots the next night.

At the time Rabbi Tzvi was studying, so he did not know about the stranger's request. His wife thought it all so unimportant that she simply forgot to tell him. The man did not come back to reclaim his boots, so they lay unclaimed and forgotten.

On the evening before Passover, Rabbi Tzvi began the customary search for any stray leavened bread. When he looked under the

bed, he found felt boots that he did not recognize. When he asked his wife about them, she suddenly remembered the stranger. Rabbi Tzvi picked up the boots to check them for bread crumbs, and found they were very heavy. Soon he realized that each boot was filled with gold coins.

Rabbi Tzvi felt this was a gift from heaven to help him realize his dream of moving to *Eretz Israel*, and immediately after Passover he and his family packed all their belongings and moved there.

All the Way to Hebron

The author of the book *Me'or Aynayim* travelled one bitter winter to visit the grave of his rabbi, the Baal Shem Tov, in Medzibozh. When he approached the grave, he took off his shoes and stood in the freezing snow. Afterwards, people asked him how he had managed to withstand such terrible cold in his socks. He answered simply, "The grave of the Baal Shem Tov is like the earth of *Eretz Israel* where it is not that cold in the winter, and I didn't feel a thing."

Face to Face

Rabbi Gershon, brother-in-law of the Baal Shem Tov, moved to *Eretz Israel*. One Friday evening the Baal Shem Tov sensed that his

brother-in-law was not in *Eretz Israel*, but by the following morning he sensed that he had returned to the country. Later, it was discovered that Rabbi Gershon had spent the Sabbath in Acre, a town which lies on the border of the historic *Eretz Israel*. On Friday evening he had prayed in a particular synagogue which was across the border, while in the morning he had prayed in one which was within the border.

The Coming of the Redeemer

Rabbi Elazar of Amsterdam made a special trip to *Eretz Israel* in order to meet Rabbi Nahman of Horodenka there, for Rabbi Nahman had said, "When both of us are present in *Eretz Israel* at the same time, the Redeemer will come."

When Rabbi Elazar arrived in Tiberias, all the elders of the town, including Rabbi Shimon, son of Rabbi Nahman, came out to meet him. Rabbi Elazar immediately asked him, "Where is your father?" "He has travelled abroad," answered Rabbi Shimon. Rabbi Elazar, in a tone of deep distress, cried out, "Woe! Woe! I came only because of him!"

When Rabbi Nahman heard that Rabbi Elazar was in *Eretz Israel*, he hurried home, but before he arrived Rabbi Elazar died.

The Maid of Ludmir

It was said that Hanah Rachel, daughter of Rabbi Manish, had within her a spark of the soul of Michal, daughter of King Saul. She studied Torah diligently, and performed many commandments from which she was exempt as a woman. She would even don the *tallit* (prayer shawl) and *tefillin* (leather boxes containing passages of the Torah and worn by men during their weekday morning prayers).

When her father died, she took her inheritance and built a synagogue. She would sit there and expound the Torah. She would say, "Had the Torah been given to women, and had women studied and taught it, the world would have been a better place." She acquired a reputation for her discourses, and soon both men and women came to hear her. The greatest sages of the generation were angered by the fact that people were coming to the

Maid of Ludmir, and forbade them to do so, but their decree was ignored.

The Maid believed that if she would but move to *Eretz Israel*, she would acquire a spark of the soul of Deborah the prophetess, and this would bring about the redemption. She moved there, and continued in the same fashion as before. When Rabbi Mordechai of Chernobyl saw that the Messiah had still not come, he sent one of his young disciples, a very handsome young man, to make her acquaintance. Soon they were married and she became a mother. Finally, the number of her Hasidim decreased, and she gradually forgot all the Torah she had known.

A Day a Year

Rabbi Moshe of Lelev had an overwhelming love for *Eretz Israel*, and desired with every fiber of his being to travel there. When everyone saw that he was seriously planning his move, both his own community and his friends, the leaders of the Hasidic groups in Galicia, tried everything possible to change his mind. Rabbi Moshe was stubborn in his resolve, and answered all those who came to entreat him, "This white beard of mine does not permit me to stay any longer."

In the first days of the summer month of Elul of the year 5610 (1850), Rabbi Moshe, his entire family, ten of his disciples and two of his attendants all set sail from one of the Rumanian ports. The ship was delayed extensively in Istanbul, Turkey, by merchants and dealers who had become aware of who Rabbi Moshe was, and who tried to extort a great deal of money from him as the price for his continuing on his voyage.

After having been stalled for over two weeks, Rabbi Moshe asked one of the merchants to try to find him a ship which was travelling to *Eretz Israel*. The merchant, who was expecting to make a large amount of money, replied that there was a plague in *Eretz Israel* among the children there, and that it was dangerous to dock there at such a time. "It may be true," replied Rabbi Moshe, "that there is a plague which affects the children in *Eretz Israel*, but here there is one which affects the adults."

Just before the beginning of the month of Heshvan, more than two months after Rabbi Moshe had left Rumania, his ship docked at Acre. As he left the ship, Rabbi Moshe told one of his close friends, "A day for each year, a day for each year." No one understood what Rabbi Moshe meant. Seventy-four days after stepping onto the shores of *Eretz Israel*, at the age of seventy-four, just as he was planning to pray at the Western Wall for the first time, Rabbi Moshe passed away in Jerusalem.

Messengers of Eretz Israel

Rabbi Avraham Yehoshua Heshel of Apta used to collect money for the needy of *Eretz Israel*, and would then give it to those messengers who had arrived from the Holy Land, for distribution there. He would greatly honor such messengers. When he found one was coming, he and all the elders of his town would go out to greet the person and escort him into the city, all the while praising his virtues. When the messenger left the town, he would again be escorted by all the elders, and the musicians would play.

Once Rabbi Avraham Yehoshua Heshel found out that the messengers were being dishonest and were pocketing some of the money for themselves. He nevertheless changed nothing in the reception he offered them. He came out with all the elders to greet them, and when they left the town, escorted them personally. The only difference was that he ordered his people to allow him to escort these messengers out of town by himself, without the elders.

As he escorted them out of town, he told them, "Do not think for an instant that you are fooling me. I know that you are keeping some of the money donated for yourselves. Why, then, do I honor you so in my town? For the small amount of money that does find its way to the poor of *Eretz Israel*. Even if a person does little for *Eretz Israel*, he deserves to be honored. The reason I alone escorted you was so that no one else might know what is happening, lest the people start contributing less to *Eretz Israel*."

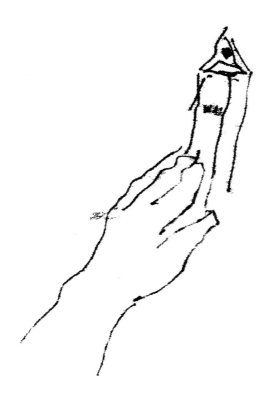

What Does Eretz Israel Produce?

Rabbi Shmuel Mohilewer once had a visitor from *Eretz Israel*. This was a source of great joy to Rabbi Shmuel, and he took the opportunity to question the visitor closely about all aspects of the country: its rebuilding, the settlements, the crops that grew there, the Torah studied within the land, and the sanctity of *Eretz Israel*.

The guest made short shrift of the various physical aspects of the country, but dwelled at length on the great sages who dwelled there and on the various holy places within the country.

After the guest had finished, Rabbi Shmuel turned to him and commented: "When the Torah (Numbers 13:20) writes of Moses' charge to the twelve spies, we are told of how he asked them to report back whether 'there are or are not trees there.' On this verse, Rashi, the medieval commentator, states that the charge was to find out 'whether there are upright people there, or not.'

"The question then arises: If Moses had been interested in finding out whether there were any upright men there, it should have stated clearly, 'Are there or aren't there any upright men there?' From this we can deduce that the text as it stands means exactly what it says, namely that it refers to trees. What Rashi is adding is that there is a second, homiletic

interpretation which refers to upright men. The first thing one must look at is *Eretz Israel* as it appears physically, *Eretz Israel* as a country."

He concluded by remarking, "Every other nation has certain holy places within *Eretz Israel*. To us the Jews, though, all of *Eretz Israel* is holy."

Maligning Eretz Israel

Once Rabbi Yaakov Shimshon of Sheptivka visited *Eretz Israel* for a time. After his stay, he decided to return to his home in order to move his family to *Eretz Israel*.

On the way home, he stopped off at an inn. When he saw himself in the mirror there, he noticed that the long and arduous journey had made him appear gaunt and pale.

He said to himself, "If I return this way after my stay in *Eretz Israel*, my friends will think that the country is unhealthy and I will thus inadvertently, Heaven forbid, be maligning it."

What did he do? He stayed in the inn for a

number of days, eating and drinking properly, until his appearance reverted back to its normal, healthy state. When he returned to his home, people thought that he looked better than when he had left, and all felt how goodly a land it was.

The Air of Eretz Israel

Once a Jew from *Eretz Israel* left the country in order to collect alms so that he could marry off his daughter. He approached Rabbi Yisrael of Rizhyn. The rabbi, seeing he was an honest man and not wanting him to remain outside *Eretz Israel* for any length of time, told him, "Go to Rabbi Meir of Primishlan, and there you will be aided."

The man arrived in Primishlan and sought lodging for the night. At that exact time, Rabbi Meir sent messengers looking for a guest from *Eretz Israel*, for he felt he could smell the air of *Eretz Israel* present. They found the man, and brought him to Rabbi Meir. He explained to Rabbi Meir how he had been sent by Rabbi Yisrael of Rizhyn. Immediately Rabbi Meir took out a bag of coins he kept under his bed and gave him all its contents, provided that he returned immediately to the Holy Land. He explained his action, saying, "While Meir loves the air of *Eretz Israel*, that air is better when it remains in its own home."

Eretz Israel Divided Between Them

Once the Baal Shem Tov was travelling from his town. As the sun began to set, he and his disciples found an inn for the night.

That evening, there was a wedding ceremony at the same inn, and all the friends and relatives of the bride and groom gathered for festivities which lasted the entire night. The Baal Shem Tov, who did not know the celebrating families, stayed in his room with his disciples.

The next morning the wedding party set out to escort the newly married couple on its way. The Baal Shem Tov also prepared to leave. As they were standing outside the inn, a little bird began to chirp. "Do you know what the bird is saying?" the Baal Shem Tov asked his disciples. They, of course, had no idea. "It is saying that 'for these, the land will be a division'" (Numbers 26:53). The disciples still could not understand their master's words, but remained silent.

As the years passed, the young couple became very wealthy, and had children and grandchildren. One day, the husband decided that he wished to move to *Eretz Israel*. The wife, though, refused adamantly, for she did not wish to leave her family. As they were unable to reconcile their differences, they turned to a rabbinic court. The court's verdict was that the wife had no legal right to prevent her husband from moving to *Eretz Israel*, while he had no right to force her to accompany him. And that is exactly how they settled the case. She stayed, while he moved to *Eretz Israel*.

This story became known throughout the Jewish world, and eventually came to the attention of the disciples of the Baal Shem Tov who had been present at the wedding. It was then that the disciples understood what their master had said so many years before, "for these, the land will be a division." *Eretz Israel* had indeed divided the two, with him moving to *Eretz Israel* and her staying in her own town.

Rabbi Nahman of Breslau's Trip to Eretz Israel

Just before Passover in the year 1798, Rabbi Nahman of Breslau proclaimed that that year he would definitely be in *Eretz Israel*. When his wife heard of this, she asked, How could he just leave them? Who would support them? He answered her, "You will travel to your father-in-law, while I will sell everything in the house to make the trip." When his family heard this, everyone began to cry, and they continued weeping for days. He had no mercy on them and told them, "Whatever happens, I will definitely make the trip, because most of myself is already there, and the minority must follow the majority."

This was in the midst of the Napoleonic wars, when Napoleon was attacking the Ottoman Empire, moving to Egypt and *Eretz Israel*. When Rabbi Nahman arrived in Istanbul, the Jews there tried to persuade him not to continue his trip, but he disregarded them.

When he finally set sail there was a great storm, and the ship ran the danger of sinking. None of the people on the ship could think of anything they might do to survive, and they all prayed aloud as if it were the Day of Atonement. While all the rest were crying out, Rabbi Nahman sat quietly. Some people approached and asked why he was not praying, but he did not answer them. Finally the wife of one of the rabbis on the ship, who had also been crying out, approached him and asked him why he was silent. He answered her, "If you all keep quiet, it will be better. I will prove it to you. If all remain silent the sea will calm down." Everyone present quieted down, and the sea turned calm.

A day or two later they ran out of water. There was a real danger that they would die of thirst. Again everyone started crying out to God, and a storm arose which twenty-four hours later deposited them in Jaffa. Rabbi Nahman wanted to leave the ship and travel to Jerusalem, but the winds were too strong for them to land in Jaffa, so they set sail for Haifa. This was two days before Rosh Hashanah, the Jewish New Year.

They finally anchored opposite Mount Carmel and Elijah's Cave, where everyone recited the *selichot* (penitential prayers) with great joy. After they completed the morning service they finally descended to the city. This was the way Rabbi Nahman finally reached his destination in the Holy Land, for which he had pined so long.

In Praise of Eretz Israel

Each Man Shall Be Born in It

The disciples of Rabbi Avraham of Kalisk complained to him of how difficult it was for them to live in *Eretz Israel*. It was so hard to earn a living, and their relatives lived so far away. What would become of them? Rabbi Avraham listened patiently, and then replied, "If you only wait a while, everything will, God willing, improve. We are told in a verse regarding *Eretz Israel* that 'each man shall be born in it.' A Jew who moves to *Eretz Israel* is as an unborn child. Once he finally settles, he becomes like a newborn, and only after sufficient time has elapsed does he begin to feel his own strength."

True Joy

Only in *Eretz Israel* can one find true joy and really sanctify oneself, something which is impossible in any other country.

What Does "Jerusalem" Mean?

Rabbi Baruch of Medzibozh explained the word "Jerusalem" as being derived from *Yira - Shalem*, meaning "perfect awe," where one achieves perfect awe of God; the place where one stands in awe of no one except of the Holy One, Blessed be He.

The Land of Yisrael

Whenever Rabbi Avraham Hazan would mention *Eretz Israel*, he would become extremely emotional, and would speak of it in awe and trembling. He used to say, "When I speak of *Eretz Israel*, I do not only refer to the land of those who keep all the commandments, but I mean the land where there is room for the most unworthy. Those who move to *Eretz Israel* – even if they do not observe the commandments and stray from the proper path – have 'strayed worthily,' because they are that much closer to the proper path."

He would also expound, "The meaning of the words *Eretz Israel* is the land which makes people into Yisrael" (a synonym for Jew).

Beloved By God

The lowliest maidservant in *Eretz Israel* is more beloved by God than the most pious righteous man outside *Eretz Israel*.

The Intention is Considered As the Deed Itself

When Rabbi Avraham Dov Auerbach of Abruch was about to leave for *Eretz Israel*, he went to bid farewell to Rabbi Aaron of Zitomir. When Rabbi Avraham Dov entered the rabbi's room, he found him to be very ill and in great pain.

After they greeted one another, Rabbi

Aaron told his guest, "In my opinion, there is one guaranteed cure for my illness – I must drink water from *Eretz Israel*. Since you are about to travel there, and all your thoughts are already directed to the Holy Land, you are considered as already living in it. Please fill me a glass of drinking water. After you take a sip, hand me the rest to finish, and I am sure I will be cured."

Rabbi Avraham Dov followed Rabbi Aaron's instructions to the letter, and in a short time Rabbi Aaron was cured.

The Fruits of the Land

Rabbi Nahman of Breslau explained the verse, "Take from the fruit (*zimrat*) of the land" (Genesis 43:11) as meaning – using another possible meaning of the word *zimrat* – "Take of the songs of the land." Jacob asked that his sons should at least take the songs of *Eretz Israel* with them, so that they would never forget the land of their forefathers. When one sings a song, one composed within the environment and landscape of *Eretz Israel*, it stirs the soul and revives the feeling of the atmosphere of the country.

The Sabbath of the Entire World

Rabbi Meir of Primishlan would send 702 gold dinars to *Eretz Israel* for distribution among the poor there. He explained to his disciples that the *gematria* (numerical value) of the word *Shabbat* (Sabbath) is 702, and *Eretz Israel* is the Sabbath of the entire world.

Five Visits

In 1921 the Rabbi of Gur, Rabbi Avraham Mordechai, left his hometown and set sail from Trieste to Jaffa for his first visit to *Eretz Israel*.

A month later, on the day before Passover, he arrived in Jerusalem, and that night held his first Passover *seder* meal in that city.

As Rabbi Avraham Mordechai reached the passage in the Haggadah of *avadim hayinu* ("We were once slaves"), he explained the passage to his students as follows: "The passage 'This year we are here, but next year we will be in *Eretz Israel*' is recited by those who live outside *Eretz Israel*, while 'This year we are slaves, next year we will be free men' is to be said by those who already live in *Eretz Israel*."

His next visit was three years later. At a meeting held in Tel Aviv with his disciples, he told them, "As you know, there are 613 commandments in the Torah, and this number parallels the total number of bones and organs in the human body. Each commandment has a specific part of the body corresponding to it, and that particular part of the body is sanctified when its commandment is performed. As the

commandment of living in *Eretz Israel* is equivalent to all the other commandments combined, by living in *Eretz Israel* one sanctifies all one's bones and organs."

Three years later he again visited *Eretz Israel*. Before embarking on the ship in Trieste, he went to a *mikveh* (ritual bath), and told his close disciples, "Before going to *Eretz Israel*, one must purify oneself in a *mikveh*."

In 1932 he visited for the fourth time. This time, instead of going by ship, he took a train which went from Vienna to Sofia, Istanbul, Aleppo, and Beirut. He explained to his disciples, "I want to know all the possible ways of entering *Eretz Israel*."

His last visit was in 1938, and he used the trip to prepare for his permanent move to the Holy Land. Due to the outbreak of the war, he was forced to remain in Poland, and was only able to make the move, with extreme effort, in the spring of 1940.

A Minor Dispute

Rabbi Tzvi of Tiberias, a grandchild of the Baal Shem Tov, once came to the Rabbi of Rizhyn. The rabbi began plying him with questions about every aspect of daily life in *Eretz Israel*. The more Rabbi Tzvi told him, the more he wished to know. Finally, Rabbi Tzvi mentioned that there had been a dispute between two tailors of a certain synagogue.

The rabbi interrupted him and said, "That news is what I was waiting for. What one must realize is that a minor dispute in *Eretz Israel* makes a greater impact on the heavenly spheres than does a major conflict between two great sages who live outside *Eretz Israel*."

The Sanctity of the Land

The first Zionist pioneers to *Eretz Israel* were mainly people who had forsaken Jewish tradition and did not fulfill the commandments.

Once a Hasid of Rabbi Moshele of Stolin mocked these new pioneers, referring to them as "the new *Eretz Israel* Jews." Rabbi Moshele, with his ever-present smile on his lips, answered him: "They certainly will not acquire anything in this world, but they will inherit the World to Come, because the sanctity of *Eretz Israel* will return them to the fold of observant Jews."

Two Wives

Rabbi Naftali Haim, the grandson of Rabbi Eliezer of Zadikov, left his wife and family and settled in *Eretz Israel* as a result of the pressures exerted by his family members in Safed and Jerusalem. After his father-in-law saw that Rabbi Naftali Haim seemed in no rush to return to his wife and children, he begged him to return to his family in Zans. When he received this request, Rabbi Naftali replied, "While my wife and children are very precious to me, I have two wives here that I cannot abandon: Zion and Jerusalem."

The Holy Land Which is Filled With Good

In his book *Edut Biyehosef*, Rabbi Yosef Sofer writes, "I must now thank God, and tell of the praises of the holy *Eretz Israel*, which has everything good in it, something which is not found in any other country. Whoever claims that it is not good to live in *Eretz Israel* is bearing false tales, just as the Ten Spies. It is important, though, that whoever comes here should bring along some money, and should not come penniless, or should be a skilled craftsman who can support himself. In this, it is like the rest of the world. Nothing is given to a person without payment."

The Jewish Intellect

"You must understand," said Rabbi Nahman of Breslau, "that there are *Eretz Israel* minds and there are the minds of other countries. The minds of the other countries are all derived from and nurtured by those of *Eretz Israel*. The primary mind and wisdom of the Jews is in *Eretz Israel*, and each Jew has a portion in the country.

"To the extent that a person has a part in *Eretz Israel*, he or she receives and is nourished by the minds of *Eretz Israel*."

A *Part of Each Other Country*

Zion is the hub and life-force of the world. It contains within itself a part of each other country. Each other land derives its life-force and nurture from its part in Zion.

A *Humble Land*

By its very nature, *Eretz Israel* makes its inhabitants submissive and humble. Thus, even though the Torah tells us of the great and mightily fortified cities that were there before it was conquered by Joshua, it was still known as Canaan, a word related to the Hebrew word *Hachna'ah*, meaning "submissiveness."

The Bread of Eretz Israel

In *Eretz Israel*, the bread is so delicious that it contains within itself the flavor of all the most delicious foods in the world.

How to Observe Eretz Israel

The Koretzer Rabbi once explained, "When Moses prayed, 'Let me go over, I pray You, and see the good land'(Deuteronomy 3:25), what he meant was that he did not want to imitate the Ten Spies who had seen only the negative aspects of *Eretz Israel*. He wanted to see its good qualities."

The Holy of Holies

When Rabbi Israel Politzker first arrived in *Eretz Israel*, he exclaimed, "At last the day has arrived which we awaited with such impatience. How happy we are here in our wonderful land, in this country which is the Holy of Holies."

The Delayed Prayers

Once, before the *minha* prayer, when the synagogue of Rabbi Menahem Mendel of Vitebsk was packed with worshippers, the rabbi went over to the window and gazed outside for a long while at the Sea of Galilee. There he remained until almost nightfall. Only afterwards did he begin his afternoon prayers.

After the Sabbath, he explained how all the prayers of the entire week are gathered together, and only on Friday afternoon, before the Sabbath, do they ascend to the heavens. The place from which the prayers of all the Jews of the Diaspora ascend is the Sea of Galilee. This week, though, the prayers had been unable to penetrate the heavenly spheres, and soon they had filled the entire area, from the ground all the way up. What had prevented them from ascending, said Rabbi Menahem, was that the Jews of the Diaspora had not been sufficiently mindful of the need to support those living in *Eretz Israel*. Only after these

Jews promised to be more mindful of their responsibility to take care of the poor of *Eretz Israel* were the prayers finally permitted to ascend to the heavens.

The Power of Eretz Israel Fruit

Once the Kobriner Rabbi visited his teacher, the Lekhovitzer Rabbi. The Lekhovitzer handed him a piece of fruit from *Eretz Israel* and quoted him the verse, "Go with the power you derive from this, and save Israel" (Judges 6:14).

Two Prayer Shawls

For a long time, Rabbi Mordechai of Neskhizh waited to receive cloth from *Eretz Israel*, so that he would be able to make a *tallit katan* (the small prayer shawl worn under one's garments) out of this holy fabric. When the cloth finally arrived, one of his students begged the rabbi for the privilege of sewing the garment. Unfortunately, the student made a mistake and, instead of cutting out one hole for the neck, cut out two such holes, spoiling the whole piece of cloth. The student was extremely upset and was terrified as to how the rabbi would react.

When he heard about what had happened, Rabbi Mordechai was not at all angry and did not berate the student. "Thank you, my son," he said. "You have done just the right thing. I really need two of these prayer shawls, one to observe the commandment and the second as a test to see whether I can control my temper."

The Festival of Exile

Rabbi Yitzhak Izaak wished very much to settle in *Eretz Israel*, and none of the attempts by his sons and friends to dissuade him could make him change his mind. Then a strange event occurred. On the evening preceding the second day of Passover, he entered the synagogue wearing his weekday *tallit* (prayer shawl) rather than his holiday *tallit*. After the evening prayers had been completed and it was time to recite the *Hallel* festive prayer, he did not begin the recitation but remained silent. Minutes passed without a word or a murmur. The congregants waited in astonishment, for the rabbi had never acted this way before. Finally Rabbi Yitzhak Izaak began and said the *Hallel* with his customary fervor.

Later, during the meal, the rabbi explained what had happened. "Today, during the prayer service," he began, "I was totally deprived of the ability to think. Not only that – I felt I was wearing my weekday *tallit*. I couldn't understand what was happening, but it finally became clear to me: because I wanted to travel to *Eretz Israel*, where the second day of the festival is not observed, I no longer had any connection to the second day of the festival. I was in the weekday world, not the festival day. When I realized what had caused me to halt, I decided that if moving to *Eretz Israel* would make me give up the special sanctity of the second day of each festival, I had to reevaluate my entire position. I thought it over carefully and decided in the end that I must renounce my plan to move to the Holy Land. Once I had made my decision, my power of thought was restored to me."

Prayers

He Raises the Lowly from the Dust Heap

Rabbi Levi Yitzhak of Berditchev was known as the defender of the Jews before God. He would always demand that God bring an end to the exile, and would offer the following prayer:

"Lord of the Universe. Why don't You act the way the most simple man of Israel acts? Once I saw a Jew, one of the most simple fellows, accidentally dropping his *tefillin* (one of the ritual leather boxes worn during prayer). He immediately bent down, picked up the *tefillin*, and kissed it fervently. Yet we, Israel, are Your *tefillin*. Close to 2000 years ago You threw us to the ground, and since that time we have been rolling in the dirt of our exile. The time has arrived, our Father in heaven, for You to raise us up from the dust and to send us the saintly Messiah."

Rabbi Simcha Bunim of Pzhysha's Prayer

Lord of the Universe! If You please, redeem Your nation Israel while they are still Jews, because if You do not do so, You will have to redeem them as non-Jews.

The Elder of Shpola's Prayer

Lord of the Universe! I swear to You that Your children, Israel, will not repent fully until You send Your righteous Messiah and redeem them completely.

Another Prayer of the Elder of Shpola

Rock of Israel! Had I not seen with my own eyes how the Jews, Your people, fulfill Your commandments and study Your Torah in this bitter and dark exile, I would not have believed it possible. I beg of You – redeem them and You will see how those who have been redeemed will serve You in *Eretz Israel*.

The Maggid of Kozhnitz's Prayer

My Father in Heaven! I ask and beg of You to redeem Your nation, Israel, and if You do not wish to redeem Your nation, then redeem the non-Jews.

A Prayer of Rabbi Nathan of Nemirov

"Out of the depths I have called the Lord; He answered me with great enlargement"(Psalms 118:4). I call upon You from the ends of the earth; lead me and have mercy upon me. Arouse Your abundant mercy and lovingkindness toward me. Aid me and enable me to speedily come to the Holy Land, which is the source of our holiness. As You know, O Lord our God, all our holiness and purity and all our Jewishness derive from *Eretz Israel*, and it is impossible to be a true Jew and to ascend from one rung of holiness to another unless we come to *Eretz Israel*, the place of our holiness, the land which You have chosen above all others and which You have given to the nation You chose above all others. This is the land which You constantly attend to, as we read, "The land which the Lord your God cares for; the Lord your God's eyes are constantly upon it, from the beginning to the end of the year" (Deuteronomy 11:12).

You know the tremendous number of problems which prevent us from going to *Eretz Israel*. We have already spent all our days and years outside the Holy Land, and we are in exile from the Land of Life and of Holiness. We are prevented from worshipping in God's inheritance, which is our life and the length of our days, and we cannot dwell on the land which You gave us.

99

Lord of the Universe! Have mercy on us in Your abundant mercy and arouse in our hearts and the hearts of our children and of all of Israel great longing for *Eretz Israel*, so that we should constantly long to come to *Eretz Israel*, until You enable us in Your great mercy to come to the Holy Land soon, so that we can be truly aroused to serve and fear You.

Have mercy on us, O He who is filled with mercy, that we should not, Heaven forbid, remain outside *Eretz Israel*, for You know all our problems and weaknesses at this time, and we are not able to eliminate the many factors which prevent our coming to *Eretz Israel*, the thousands and tens of thousands of problems which we are unable to overcome. Only with the help of Your great strength and Your abundant mercy can we overcome these factors, and we have no one to lean upon except You, our Father in Heaven.

Have mercy upon Your nation Israel and bring us speedily to *Eretz Israel*, and give me the strength in Your great mercy to be victorious in the battle to destroy and banish and annul all those who spread false tales about *Eretz Israel*, who cause all types of impediments for those wishing to come to *Eretz Israel*, so that we will be able to come speedily and in peace to *Eretz Israel*.

A Prayer of Rabbi Nachman

Please, O God, in Your goodness aid me, and grant me in mercy and undeservedly the means to be able to come to *Eretz Israel* soon, to the Holy Land, the land which our forefathers inherited, the land which all the truly righteous longed for. Most of those who came there and improved what they improved and accomplished what they accomplished and achieved what they achieved did so entirely by the sanctity of *Eretz Israel*, which is the focal point of all holiness in the world.

O Lord, make me, through Your abundant mercy, long for and desire with a true desire to come to *Eretz Israel* soon – for You know how great my need is, and how much I must be in *Eretz Israel*.

The Sanctity of Eretz Israel

Why Not Jerusalem?

It is told that Rabbi Yisrael of Rizhyn was bothered by a question: Why was it that the Hasidim who moved to *Eretz Israel* settled primarily in the Galilee and not Jerusalem?

None of the conventional answers satisfied him, so he finally asked Rabbi Moshe of Kobrin, "Why is it that Rabbi Menahem Mendel of Vitebsk did not settle in Jerusalem, site of the Temple, and established the Hasidic movement in Safed and Tiberias?"

Rabbi Moshe replied simply, "Rabbi Menahem Mendel feared the sanctity of Jerusalem."

We Must Sanctify the Land

A Hasidic rabbi explained, "Once *Eretz Israel* was sanctified, and it sanctified everyone who lived in it. Now the land has sunk low, and we must be the ones to sanctify it again. This can only be achieved by a sanctified person, such as Rabbi Menahem Mendel."

Proper Intentions

Whoever is really sincere and travels to *Eretz Israel* in order to return to God, will find that *Eretz Israel* helps him or her greatly. Even the very fact of entering *Eretz Israel* makes him or her a more holy person.

On the other hand, if such people have no

desire whatsoever to serve God and to destroy the evil within themselves, living in *Eretz Israel* will not help them. Instead, the land will reject them.

The Gates of Light

Rabbi Yitzhak Izaak of Ziditzov always wanted to move to *Eretz Israel*. Why, then, did he not do so? He did not wish to forgo the second day of the different holidays, which is only celebrated outside *Eretz Israel*. He nevertheless built a synagogue in the holy town of Safed.

He used to say that each day he visited *Eretz Israel*. When he studied the sacred text of the Zohar and found himself unable to understand a particularly difficult passage, he would lay his head on the charity box for *Eretz Israel*, the charity of Rabbi Meir Baal Haness, until he felt he understood the passage which had been troubling him. He explained that what he did was in keeping with the saying of our Sages that "the air of *Eretz Israel* makes one wise."

Eretz Israel is Like the Sabbath

In his volume *Divrei Aaron*, Rabbi Aaron of Karlin writes, "*Eretz Israel* is like the Sabbath. Just as the Sabbath remains a holy day in spite of the fact that there are people who violate its rules, *Eretz Israel* does not cease to be holy because there are those who violate its rules."

The Divine Presence

Eretz Israel is the Shechina, the Divine Presence.

The Tzaddik And Eretz Israel

Rabbi Aaron of Kaidanov used to say, "Our era, beginning with the Baal Shem Tov, is the era of the Messiah. Just as in our time people are accustomed to travel to the Tzaddik (the title bestowed upon a Hasidic leader), so too will the Tzaddikim travel to *Eretz Israel*. And whatever people can accomplish by visiting a Tzaddik will also be accomplished in *Eretz Israel*. *Eretz Israel* has the attributes of a Tzaddik."

Is Eretz Israel Really Different?

Rabbi Nahman of Breslau once said, "When I was in *Eretz Israel*, I heard from prominent people there that before they had come to *Eretz Israel*, they couldn't imagine that it belongs to our world. Based on what they had read in the holy books about its sanctity, they were convinced that it was entirely on a different plane. However, after they came to *Eretz Israel*, they found that it is indeed of this world. Its earth is just like the earth of all the countries from which they came. Its outward appearance is no different than that of other countries – and yet, it is the most holy of all countries. This is similar to the truly righteous person, the Tzaddik, who appears outwardly to be the same as everyone else. The Tzaddik nevertheless is different, but only those who believe in him can sense his holiness. In the same way, only those who believe in the sanctity of *Eretz Israel* can feel its holiness and can realize that its skies are different."

Being Truly a Jew

Whoever really wishes to be a Jew – which means one who wishes to constantly ascend from one level of holiness to another – can only accomplish this in *Eretz Israel*. I refer here to *Eretz Israel* in the simple, material sense, with its homes and apartments.

Even though we have been praying for so many years to return to *Eretz Israel* and are still so far from it, we must know that every single cry and prayer, be it of the most simple person, is never lost, for every cry and prayer conquers for us a part of *Eretz Israel*.

The Natural And the Miraculous

Outside *Eretz Israel*, a person who succeeds does so by natural means. In *Eretz Israel*, on the other hand, a special Divine blessing is also present, which is beyond the natural state of affairs.

The Air of Eretz Israel

Rabbi Menahem used to say, "It is true that the air of *Eretz Israel* makes one more wise. As long as I was outside the country, my only desire was to be able to say a single solitary prayer with the proper devotion. Now that I am in *Eretz Israel*, the only request in my heart is that I will at least once answer 'Amen' in the proper fashion."

He also said, "I accomplished one thing in *Eretz Israel*. When I walk down the road and see a bundle of straw lying parallel to the road and not perpendicular to it, in my eyes that is a sign of God's Divine Presence, for nothing in *Eretz Israel* happens without Divine intervention."

Eretz Israel's Appearance

Externally, there is no discernible difference between *Eretz Israel* and other countries. It is nevertheless of the greatest holiness. Happy is he or she who walks four cubits in it.

From the Sacred to the Profane

Once the Rabbi of Medzibozh was given a bottle of *Eretz Israel* wine. He asked his son, "What should we drink when we finish this bottle?" "Our normal wine," was the reply. "Then take away the *Eretz Israel* wine right now," the rabbi commanded his son. "Once one has drunk sacred wine at a meal, it would be profane to drink normal wine."

A Guaranteed Gift

Rabbi Bunim explained, "We are told in a verse (Nehemiah 9:8) that 'You made a covenant with him to give him the land of the Canaanite ... to give it to him and his descendants.' The reason the words 'to give' are repeated twice is to indicate that God guaranteed His gift by giving it to a holy nation to live in it."

Speaking Hebrew

The Jews living in *Eretz Israel* must speak the Holy Tongue, which is the holy language that was used in creating the world. If the Jews there do not speak Hebrew, the land will not belong to them, and it will be simple to exile them from it. The land is ours because we speak the Holy Tongue.

Moving to Eretz Israel

Banished to Eretz Israel

On the *seder* night of Passover, the year before Rabbi Yisrael of Rizhyn died, he was seated at the traditional Passover *seder* meal of the Maggid of Mezritch. He wore the white *kittel* (robe) which had belonged to his grandfather, the *Malach*, Rabbi Avraham. When they reached the paragraph in the *seder* of *vihi she'amda*, telling of how God's promises had sustained the Jews throughout their history, he stopped at the words, "there have been many who have attempted to destroy us," and repeated them over and over. Finally, he looked up and turned to his family, saying:

"Before the Messiah comes, all the nations of the world will hate us violently. After they finally realize that all their persecution has not helped to rid them of us, they will banish us to *Eretz Israel*. Then we will see wonders: a nation which has suffered throughout with forced labor and exile will not be willing to free itself voluntarily, and they will be forced to banish us from their countries. The main thing, though, is that we return to our own country."

The Baal Shem Tov's Disciples

After the disciples of the Baal Shem Tov realized that their master would never make the move to *Eretz Israel*, they decided that it was their duty to do so, and thus hasten God's

ultimate redemption. As Rabbi Nahman of Horodenka and Rabbi Menahem Mendel of Primishlan were sailing on the ocean on their way to the Holy Land, a great storm arose, and the ship ran the danger of sinking.

At that point Rabbi Nahman went up on deck, carrying a Torah scroll, and proclaimed: "If, God forbid, we have been sentenced to die, it will not happen on a ship bound for *Eretz Israel*. We, the *beth din* (religious court) convened here, do not accept such a verdict. We do not want people to impugn *Eretz Israel* by saying that people die on their way to it." They all recited verses of the Psalms with great fervor, and soon the storm abated.

113

Rabbi Menahem Mendel had the privilege of settling in the holy city of Jerusalem, where he spent all his time studying the Torah and praying for the redemption. He used to say, "Before I arrived in *Eretz Israel*, I always used to hope that one day I would say at least one prayer with the proper devotion. Now that I live in *Eretz Israel*, where the very air makes one wise, I desire only to say a single word with the proper fervor." And there are those who say that on his deathbed Rabbi Menahem Mendel begged only that he be able to say a single letter in the proper manner.

Protection on the High Seas

Before Rabbi Avraham Dov of Abruch, author of *Bat Ayin*, travelled to *Eretz Israel*, he came to his rabbi, Rabbi Mordechai of Chernobyl, to request his blessing, and to have a guard made available to him for the ocean voyage. Rabbi Mordechai replied that there was already a guard waiting for him at Odessa, the seaport from which he was to set sail.

When Rabbi Avraham Dov arrived in Odessa, he asked all his friends and acquaintances there if anyone knew of any guard who should be awaiting him. No one knew anything about it. He waited a week, two weeks, and still there were no signs of a guard. Finally, he decided to leave by himself.

On the trip, Rabbi Avraham Dov was approached by a poor man who asked for charity. Seeing that the man was indeed worthy, Rabbi Avraham Dov offered him two gold coins. The man refused this amount, and requested a coin named a Randel. Unfortunately, Rabbi Avraham Dov explained, as he was travelling to *Eretz Israel*, he had few coins with him, and did not have one like that. The poor man left. The next day he returned, again asked for a donation, and was again offered the two coins, which he refused. And the same happened every single day of the trip.

When they arrived in *Eretz Israel*, the man told Rabbi Avraham Dov that in reality he did not need any money. Rabbi Mordechai of Chernobyl had sent him along to supply protection to him on the ocean, for the greatest protection he had was in mentioning *Eretz Israel* each day.

Who Should Move to Eretz Israel?

The Savraner Rabbi remarked, "A person who serves God completely and despises worldly affairs should if possible live in *Eretz Israel*. The holiness of the land will enable him or her to attain an even higher level of sanctity.

"On the other hand, if a person has not yet been separated from worldliness and is not devoted totally to the service of God, it will be better for him or her to remain outside *Eretz Israel*. In general, God has made the holy and unholy forces equal in power in the battle for people's souls. In *Eretz Israel*, where the degree of sanctity is that much higher, the Evil Impulse is proportionately that much stronger, and a person who has not mastered his or her drives and impulses will find it that much harder to resist."

Let the Children Move to Eretz Israel

When Rabbi Menahem Mendel of Kotzk's disciples came to him to request permission to move to *Eretz Israel*, he told them, "I never realized how much you care for your own selves." In general, Rabbi Menahem Mendel did not advise his disciples to move to *Eretz Israel*, telling them, "Haven't you sinned enough in your own homes that you wish to sin in the palace of the King? In your youth, when you would have been able to be involved in the rebuilding and settling of the land, you did not make the move. Now that you are old and weak, you wish to go to *Eretz Israel*. The Torah has already informed us that 'your carcasses will die in this desert.' If you really wish to fulfill a commandment, send your children to *Eretz Israel*."

To what Lengths Must one Go?

Many of the greatest and saintliest people went through all types of trials and tribulations, as well as being exposed to all kinds of danger, until they finally managed to arrive in *Eretz Israel*. How much more should this be true for us, who are but nothings. We should be willing to wallow in the mud and roll in the dust – even among snakes and scorpions – until we are finally able to attain *Eretz Israel* and to breathe its holy and awesome air.

The Return

Rabbi Bunim explained the verse, "Trust in the Lord and observe His ways, and He will exalt you to inherit the land" (Psalms 37:34) as follows: the Lord tells us that the Jews have first to achieve fame among the nations before they are able to inherit *Eretz Israel*. The Jews must therefore become so great that they will arouse the admiration of the other nations, and then they will be ready to return to their own land.

The Old Mother

When Rabbi Shmuel Meir immersed himself in the Torah teachings of Rabbi Nahman of Breslau, he left the town of Uman and travelled to *Eretz Israel*. On the way he encountered many obstacles, some normal and some abnormal

ones, but he managed to overcome them and finally arrived at the port of Trieste in Italy. Right then there was a ship ready to leave for *Eretz Israel*, but he was short ten florins of the amount needed to pay the fare. He was very distressed, and as he walked along, barefoot and hungry, he prayed: "Lord of the Universe! You know how much I desire to be in *Eretz Israel* and how much effort it required for me to arrive here. Now that there is a ship travelling to my destination, shall I not go on it?" He felt someone touch his shoulder, and before he had a chance to turn around, heard a young man saying to him, "Sir, are you travelling to *Eretz Israel*? I have an old mother there, and I would appreciate if you bring her these ten florins. Have a good journey." The young man handed him the ten florins and left. And so Rabbi Shmuel Meir reached the Holy Land.

Follow in the Footsteps of Your Rabbi

Before Rabbi Moshele of Lelev departed for *Eretz Israel*, he came to bid farewell to Rabbi Shlomo Hakohen of Radomsk, and told him, "You, rabbi, are a *kohen*, a member of the priestly clan descended from Aaron, the first High Priest. Please bless me before I travel to *Eretz Israel*." Rabbi Shlomo answered him, "A *kohen* who blesses others is in turn blessed by God."

When Rabbi Moshele's Hasidim realized that their rabbi was serious and was going to leave them, they began crying and asked him, "Rabbi, you are leaving us as a flock without a shepherd. Who will take care of us?" He answered them, "Travel to Rabbi Shlomo of Radomsk." When they came to Rabbi Shlomo, he chased them away, saying, "Follow in the footsteps of your rabbi."

A Tale of Three Breslau Hasidim

Once three Hasidim of Breslau sailed to *Eretz Israel* to live there. They had neither silver nor gold nor the necessary papers, for this was still a time when the non-Jewish government felt it had, as it were, the right to prevent Jews from living in their ancestral home.

After each prayer on the ship, the three would break out into a joyful dance, and would make everyone with them rejoice. The other

immigrants could not understand why they were so joyful. In fact, everyone else was very concerned for them, sure that they would be deported as soon as the ship docked.

When the ship arrived at the port, the three Breslau Hasidim were the first to disembark. The government officials who were present read off their names from a list, and ordered that they be the first ones to be admitted into the country. One of the people present, who was normally involved in aiding Jews in distress, was astounded. He had been counting on trying to intercede for the three, and suddenly there was nothing left for him to do. He came over to the Hasidim and told them, "There has obviously been an error. Leave this place as

soon as possible, before the authorities realize
their mistake and put you back on the ship."
As they saw the man meant well, the three
took his advice and left immediately.

Some time later this man met the three
Hasidim at the Western Wall, and remarked,
"You were granted a miracle. Please tell me
about it." They answered him, "What is there
to tell? Our God is great. Our rabbi is great,
and *Eretz Israel* is great." The writer of this
story added, "I heard this story from one of the
Breslau Hasidim. He told me that he had heard
it from a person who was not a Hasid. That
man told him that after having seen this event
with his own eyes, he would always stand up
whenever a Breslau Hasid entered the room."

A Difficult And Dangerous Trip

When Rabbi Moshe of Lelev decided to move to *Eretz Israel*, a family crisis resulted. His wife, Rivka Rachel, the daughter of the *Yehudi Hakadosh* (the Holy Jew) of Pzhysha, was adamantly opposed to her husband leaving his position as the rabbi of Pshidburz, and in spite of all his pleading and entreating, she insisted on remaining in Poland and not moving with him.

Rabbi Moshe, though, insisted that his daughter-in-law, Matil, accompany her husband and himself on their journey to the Holy Land. Her parents were concerned for her health, and did not want her to endanger herself by undertaking such an arduous, long and dangerous journey, as it was at that time. Rabbi Moshe was uncompromising, and told her father, Rabbi Tzvi Horowitz, that "either your daughter comes with us, or she accepts a divorce." In order to end the dispute, both families agreed to travel to Rabbi Shalom of Belz, whose verdict they all agreed would be binding.

After the different sides had presented their cases, Rabbi Shalom turned to them and told them that neither side could determine whether Matil would travel or not. This decision was strictly hers alone, and she should thus be called upon to make her own decision.

When the young woman entered the chambers of Rabbi Shalom, the Rabbi explained to her the difficulties involved in the journey, and then asked her, "Are you willing to travel under such circumstances?" The young woman immediately answered, "Travelling to the rabbi also involves pain and great difficulty, nevertheless people are willing to make a sacrifice and do come to him. The holy *Eretz Israel* is surely no less important than the rabbi." She thus agreed to leave her home and made the trip with her husband and his family.

"Shall I Leave My Children?"

One of the Hasidim of Rabbi Yitzhak of Boyan approached the rabbi and asked whether he might be permitted to move to *Eretz Israel*. "How about your children? Will they be coming with you?" the rabbi asked. "Unfortunately they cannot do so," the Hasid answered. "Their money is tied up in real estate, and they don't have the money available for the move." "If that is the case," the rabbi told him, "then you are not to go either. Your children need you to guide them in the proper path. Let me illustrate my point. God loves Zion and has chosen Jerusalem. Nevertheless, as long as His children are in exile, He stays with them, and the *Shechina* (God's presence) remains in exile with them."

Worthy of Moving to Eretz Israel

In *Pitgamin Kadishin Hashalem*, a collection of aphorisms, we find the following:

"Only those who observe the commandments of God properly will be able to move to *Eretz Israel*. Those people who are ignorant of their Creator, and who do not wish to observe His commandments in their homes, who do not study the Torah, do not check to be sure that the *mezuzot* (parchment inscribed with specific Biblical verses) on their doors are in order, do not give charity, and so on, will certainly not be able to move to *Eretz Israel*, because they are not pleasing to God here, outside *Eretz Israel*. Only those who are pleasing to God by their behavior will be able to move to *Eretz Israel*."

The Anonymous Tombstone

Throughout his life, Rabbi Haim of Krasna tried to move to *Eretz Israel*, but he was never able to do so. Once, when he had finally set sail, his ship was capsized in a storm and he was only rescued by a miracle. Unfortunately, his rescuers returned him to his original home rather than to *Eretz Israel*, and this caused him great anguish for the rest of his days. Before he died he requested that his tombstone was to contain no words of praise or titles, because he had failed in his efforts to move to *Eretz Israel*.

In the Dust Heap

Before Rabbi Mendel moved to *Eretz Israel*, he went to his rabbi, Rabbi Yaakov Yosef of Polnoye, to say goodbye. He arrived at the inn in a carriage pulled by three horses, and this infuriated the Hasidim, who had been trained by their rabbi to disdain any sign of ostentation. They were even more angry when he came out from the inn wearing only a *yarmulke* (skullcap) rather than the hat everyone else wore, and was smoking a pipe, as he entered the Rabbi's quarters. They were sure that Rabbi Yaakov Yosef, who was known to have a fiery temper, would soon evict Rabbi Mendel because of his conduct. Instead, the rabbi came out of his home to greet the guest personally, escorted him inside, and spent hours talking to him in private.

After Rabbi Mendel had left, the Hasidim asked their rabbi, "Rabbi, why were you so gracious to this man, when he came without a hat, with silver buckles on his shoes, and smoking a long pipe?" The rabbi explained, "When a king goes out to do battle, he hides all his treasures in various safe places. However, he takes his most valuable jewels and buries them in the sand, because he is sure no one will look for them there. In the same manner, Rabbi Mendel hid his true humility in the dust heap of ostentatious behavior, so that the powers of evil will not be able to harm him."

Preparing for the Move to Eretz Israel

"God said to Abraham: 'Go forth from your country and from your homeland and from the home of your father to the place which I will show you'" (Genesis 12:1).

Rabbi Zusya of Hanipol would explain the verse in the following manner: "'Go forth from your country' – leave your own contamination.
'And from your homeland' – and that which your mother instilled in you.
'And from the home of your father' – and that instilled by your father.

"Only after you have discarded all the contamination within you, when you have been sanctified and are clean of sin, can you go to the place which I will show you."

The First Commandment

Rabbi Meir Yehiel of Ostrowiec explained that the commandment to Abraham to "go forth ... to the place that I will show you" (Genesis 12:1) was the first commandment ever dictated to a Jew, and as such the commandment to live in *Eretz Israel* is a very important one.

The only Ascent

Rabbi Meir Simha of Dvinsk commented that the Jewish people are only worthy of their special place in Creation when they are in their own homeland, the land where they were conceived, and which is protected constantly by God.

If any Jew claims that he or she is "ascending" to any other country, he or she is lying, because a Jew can only ascend to the land promised to our forefathers.

What We Can Do

Rabbi Haim Tzvi Shneersohn declared, "we must all unite under a single covenant to ascend to Jerusalem and take possession of our land.

"In His great wisdom, God decreed that the redemption will come about gradually. We must do whatever we possibly can, and then we hope that God will add to our efforts and aid us."

Really Wanting to Move to Eretz Israel

Whoever wants to truly be a Jew must travel to *Eretz Israel*. If there are many factors which prevent it, he or she must abolish these factors and go there, for that is the primary victory in the battle.

It is impossible to come to *Eretz Israel* without travail.

There are those who think they really want and desire to come to *Eretz Israel* – provided they can make the move in comfort, but not in want or with great effort. That is not real desire, because anyone who truly wishes to move to *Eretz Israel* must go there on foot, just as Abraham was commanded, "Go (literally "walk") to the land I will show you" – he was specifically commanded to walk there.

Whenever I travel anywhere – my destination is always *Eretz Israel*.

Whoever is really sincere and travels to *Eretz Israel* in order to return to God, will find that *Eretz Israel* helps greatly in this quest.

Turning Back on the Way to Eretz Israel

Rabbi Elimelech of Lizhensk, a disciple of the Maggid, decided to move to *Eretz Israel*. He went as far as Brody, but there his conscience bothered him for having left his Hasidim without a leader. He immediately decided to return home.

Two Returns

Rabbi Meir Simha of Dvinsk was puzzled by a verse in Deuteronomy (30:3), which states that "The Lord your God will return your exile and have mercy on you. He will return and gather you from among all the other nations." "Why," he asked, "does the verse imply two separate acts of return?" To answer his question, he explained the process of the ultimate redemption.

In the first stage, God will return those who always longed for *Eretz Israel*, whose hearts yearned to return to it. These are the ones that God will have mercy on and whom He will bring to *Eretz Israel*. His actions will stem from His feelings of pity for the longing and anguish that these people suffer in not being in *Eretz Israel*.

After that stage has been completed, God will continue to gather in the exiles, but this time He will bring those who have had no desire to return, who have felt comfortable living in foreign lands.

An Equation

Rabbi Yisrael of Rizhyn exclaimed, "The trip that Rabbi Mendel made to *Eretz Israel* was equivalent to that made by our father Abraham to that country. Both wished to blaze a path for God and for the Jewish people."

Amazed At the Words of the Sages

Rabbi Yosef Sofer wrote in one of his letters, "I have already written to you from Istanbul that when I wanted to board the ship, the sages and notables of the city summoned me to the assembly hall, where they used to meet each Wednesday to enact local decrees. They told me, 'We would like to ask you to stay for a few years. Why are you in such a hurry to travel to

Eretz Israel? If you make your home here, you will earn a fine salary, something you cannot do in *Eretz Israel*.'

"I answered them, 'I am amazed at such scholars as you. Do you think I came to earn money? My only aim has been to move to *Eretz Israel*, and not to save money. Who knows what tomorrow will bring? I am convinced that the same God who has not abandoned me until now will also help me in *Eretz Israel*.' When they heard that, they all offered a blessing that I should go in peace, and that God should enable me to arrive in *Eretz Israel*."

Letters from Eretz Israel

An Appeal

In a letter sent after he had moved to *Eretz Israel* in 1777, Rabbi Yisrael of Polotsk appealed to the Jews in other countries to aid those living in *Eretz Israel*. He wrote:

"My fellow-Jews, who are merciful and perform kind deeds: It is both your task and ours to rebuild the House of our God, and therefore all Jews must aid in the settling of *Eretz Israel*. Take note of the souls of your unfortunate brothers who were ready to die, and who have undergone all types of agonies. Strengthen your hands and gird yourselves. Arise and arouse others to aid in this great commandment of enabling a large body of Jews to continue living, by giving them food and drink, and clothing the naked. They then will be able to return to the Holy Land and arouse the mercy of the Supreme One, as they pray for all of Israel. Remember that you too are a partner in *Eretz Israel*.

"Whoever has true fear of God in his or her heart should exert all effort, physical and financial, to enlist aid for these Jews, so that mercy will be shown to the remnants of those living there, who pray and beseech God to bring peace to our precious land, so that there will be peace for all Jews. May God gather us soon and may we all come together to walk in God's light to Zion, to the house of the God of Jacob."

How Long Are You Going to Live Outside Eretz Israel?

In a letter to his brother, Rabbi Menahem of Primishlan wrote, "How long will you remain outside *Eretz Israel*? All you hear is those who spread evil tales about the Holy Land by worthless people.

"One must pray extensively to appreciate its holiness, and then you will know clearly that you are walking with God."

The Emissary

In a letter which he sent from Safed in 1781, Rabbi Menahem Mendel of Vitebsk wrote, "I am in the Holy Land as an emissary of the various countries to the palace of the King. Nothing escapes my attention regarding the proper operation of the country, in both its physical and spiritual dimensions."

A Transformation

In a letter describing how the Hasidim came to *Eretz Israel* and the changes they made in the country, Rabbi Yisrael of Politzk writes:

"The Holy Land, praised by our forefathers – all left it and wandered elsewhere, so that it remained desolate, without inhabitants. It was barren and waste, without its children ...

"Now, it is blessed with abundance, as a

nation is reborn in it. We found in it large and fine houses – but no one lived in them.

"This is the day for which we have longed; let us rejoice in our precious land, the treasure of our hearts, the joy of our thoughts, the most sanctified of all sanctities."

The Difference

When he had returned from his visit to *Eretz Israel*, Rabbi Nahman of Breslau wrote:

"Materially, in the eyes of man, one sees no difference between *Eretz Israel* and the other countries. Only one who is able to believe in its sanctity can perceive a slight difference.

"All of my vigor stems from those days I spent in *Eretz Israel*. Proof of this is that when Jacob sent his sons to Joseph in Egypt, he had them take along a song of *Eretz Israel* (to sustain them), as we see in the verse (Genesis 43:11), 'Take from *zimrat ha'aretz*' (which can be translated not only as 'the fruit of the land,' but also as 'the song of the land')."

Redemption of the Land

What We Can Do

Rabbi Haim Tzvi Shneersohn declared, "We must all unite under a single covenant to ascend to Jerusalem and take possession of our land.

"In His great wisdom, God decreed that the redemption will come about gradually. We must do whatever we possibly can, and then we hope that God will add to our efforts and aid us."

The Land of Abraham

The Kozmirer Rabbi said, "The Lord gave Canaan to Abraham provided that his heirs would follow in his footsteps. When his son Ishmael did not adhere fully to his father's teachings, the other son, Isaac, inherited the land. When Isaac's son Esau did not comply with the true tradition, his brother Israel (another name for Jacob) received the heritage.

"When Israel became habitually delinquent, his heirloom reverted to Esau (Rome and Christendom). When Esau's followers degenerated, they were compelled to surrender Canaan to Ishmael (the Muslims).

"Now the process is reversing itself. The land was lost by Ishmael to Edom (Esau), and will shortly return to its rightful owner, Israel."

Interpreting a Verse

On the verse, "The Children of Israel went out (of Egypt) with a high hand" (Exodus 14:8), the Targum (Aramaic translation) renders this as *b'reish galei*, or "in full public view." Rabbi Haim of Sadylkov, the grandson of the Baal Shem Tov, took the word *b'reish* as being a mnemonic for *B'reish Reb Yisrael* ("under the leadership of Rabbi Yisrael" – the first name of the Baal Shem Tov), i.e., only when Rabbi Yisrael's teachings will have spread throughout the world will the Jews finally be led out of exile.

The Importance of Supporting Eretz Israel

You no doubt know or have heard of the great importance of the commandment to strengthen the settlement in *Eretz Israel*. After all, our sages permitted profaning the Sabbath even to acquire a single house in the country. Imagine then the importance of keeping a number of pure souls there alive, ones who serve God in holiness and purity.

Adding a Brick

The Roptchitzer Rabbi stated, "By our service of God we build Jerusalem each day. One of us adds a row, another only a single brick. When Jerusalem is completed, the redemption will come."

Love of the Land

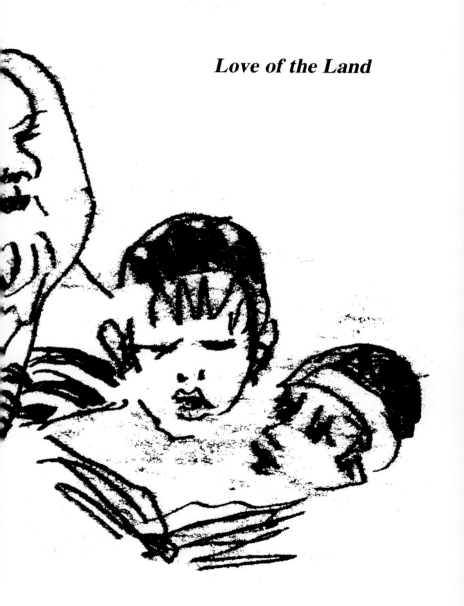

The Rabbi's Concern

Rabbi Yohanan of Rachmistrivska once received a bottle of wine from *Eretz Israel*, but refused to drink it. His explained his refusal simply: "I do not know whether I will like this particular bottle of wine. Since I do not want, heaven forbid, to possibly disparage something which comes from *Eretz Israel*, I would rather not drink the bottle."

Money to Eretz Israel

Rabbi Shneur Zalman of Ladi, author of the Tanya, was always engaged in aiding or causing others to aid *Eretz Israel*. He said, "Whoever cannot fulfill the commandment by actually living in *Eretz Israel* should fulfill it by donating money to it, and whoever has no money should spend the effort in collecting money from others for *Eretz Israel*."

Even though Rabbi Shneur Zalman was falsely accused of various crimes and had to defend himself against these accusations, he in no way lessened his efforts for *Eretz Israel*. Were there those who talked against him? So what! It is a good sign when people complain about a person. Didn't the Jews criticize Moses?

Each year, Rabbi Shneur Zalman would send a special messenger carrying money to *Eretz Israel*. And these were his instructions to the messenger: "You are to bring the money to *Eretz Israel*. If you find Jews there, give them the money. If there are no Jews, give the money to Arabs. And if you find no man there, throw it away on the mountains. Undoubtedly people will eventually come there who will need it."

Rabbi Shneur Zalman was privileged to write his major work, the *Tanya*, of which Rabbi Levi Yitzhak of Berditchev said, "This is the work of a Jew with sense! He enclosed a great God in a small book, so that Jews can then enclose that God in their hearts."

The Love of Eretz Israel

Rabbi Pinhas of Koretz used to say, "*Eretz Israel* used to be beautiful because the Jews lived in it. When the Jews were exiled, both the land and its people lost their beauty. It is thus

incumbent on every Jew to return to *Eretz Israel* and to return the country to its former beauty."

Rabbi Pinhas carried in his mind a vivid picture of *Eretz Israel* in all its beauty and splendor, and throughout his life he attempted to move and live there.

Whenever a messenger from *Eretz Israel* would arrive, Rabbi Pinhas would postpone whatever else he was doing and give him his undivided attention. He would ask question after question, detail upon detail, and thirstily drink in every new scrap of information.

He used to say, "In any country ruled by a king, the districts in closest proximity to the king require the least protection from enemies, because the king has direct control over them. Only the outlying districts require a great deal

of protection. We are told in the Torah that 'God's eyes are constantly upon' *Eretz Israel*, and there can be no greater protection than that."

Toward the end of his life he set out to move to *Eretz Israel*, but died on the trip. His death made a great impact on those living in *Eretz Israel*. Here was a person who had devoted his life to *Eretz Israel*, but who had not lived to see it. How mysterious are the ways of God.

Eretz Israel Protects the Jews

It was said that all his life Rabbi Yerahmiel of Koznitz dreamed of *Eretz Israel*. He used to say, "The Torah forbids one to be jealous of others, and thank God I am not jealous of a soul, except of those Jews who travel to *Eretz Israel*."

Whenever he received a letter from *Eretz Israel*, he would guard it zealously in a special box set aside for such items, and which he referred to as "the holy box."

He used to say, "I learned my love of *Eretz Israel* from Rabbi Aaron of Karlin, who used to announce, '*Eretz Israel* is like the Sabbath. Just as the Sabbath protects the Jewish people, *Eretz Israel* also protects the Jewish people.'"

The Holiness of Eretz Israel

After Rabbi Avraham Hazan had moved to *Eretz Israel* from Uman, he said, "In Uman I learned of the sanctity of *Eretz Israel*, and in *Eretz Israel* I learned of the sanctity of Uman."

Each year Rabbi Avraham would travel to Uman for Rosh Hashanah (the Jewish New Year). He would bring with him a bottle of wine from *Eretz Israel*, and each time he drank a cup of any wine, he would add a drop of the wine of *Eretz Israel*, so that the drink might acquire a little of the taste and sanctity of *Eretz Israel*. He hoarded that bottle very carefully, so that it might last him all the time until he returned to *Eretz Israel*. It is said that Rabbi Avraham once remarked, "In the future Uman will expand to all of *Eretz Israel*, and there will be no need for a Jew to ever leave *Eretz Israel*."

The Joy of Eretz Israel

Rabbi Yitzhak of Neskhizh was constantly in pain, yet was never despondent. Instead, he was always joyful and made others cheer up. He would preach against sadness and in praise of those who kept away from it. He used to say, "Sadness is what keeps redemption away from us, for *Eretz Israel* is entirely light and joy, and awaits those happy ones who will come and rebuild it."

He would expound, "The Jews are referred to by ten different phrases expressing joy, while exile is referred to by ten different expressions of sadness. When the Jews overcome the despondency of exile and redeem *Eretz Israel*, they will be referred to by twenty different expressions of joy and redemption."

The Will

When Rabbi Moshe Hamburger decided to move to *Eretz Israel* with his wife and children, his friends tried to dissuade him, telling him that there was no work available in the country, and how would he support his family? He answered them, "It is a land flowing with milk and honey."

He became enamored of the land, and the land became enamored of him, and they signed a mutual covenant of love binding the one to the other. In his will, he commanded his children "never to leave *Eretz Israel* for any length of time or for any reason, except for medical treatment." In order to ensure that the children might not use this as a loophole, for there were many temptations to leave the land, he added,"This need is to be established by a proper and expert *beth din* (court of Jewish law) in Jerusalem."

Holy Paper

When the first Hasidim of Breslau would receive a letter from *Eretz Israel*, they would kiss it with great love, and place it in the bag of their *tefillin* (the ritual leather boxes worn during weekday morning prayers). They explained their action as follows: "The *tefillin* are holy, and so are these letters which come from *Eretz Israel*. It is proper that a holy object be kept with other holy objects."

When one of the Hasidim died, they always attempted to place some of the earth of *Eretz Israel* in the grave. When no such earth was available, they would place these letters in the grave instead, for this was paper that had actually been in *Eretz Israel*, and which had been written upon by a person in *Eretz Israel*.

The Will of a Rabbi

In his will Rabbi Menahem Mendel of Vitebsk, who was later buried in *Eretz Israel*, wrote:

"The pallbearers are to place my body directly into the grave; not on boards but directly touching the holy earth. When they cover my eyes with pottery pieces, as is the custom, they are to mention our teacher, the Baal Shem Tov, and the Maggid (the disciple of the Baal Shem Tov). All my clothes, both weekday and festive, including my coat with silver buttons, are to be distributed to the poor."

The Envelope is Holy

The "Elder," Rabbi Aaron of Chernobyl, devoted much time and attention to establishing a synagogue in Safed. Once when a messenger came from there carrying with him a letter about the state of the building, Rabbi Aaron asked everyone else to leave his room, so that he could give the messenger his undivided attention. As soon as the man entered the room, Rabbi Aaron eagerly took the letter from his hand. In his haste, he opened the envelope, took out the letter, and let the envelope slip out of his hand. As soon as he realized what had happened, he bent down, picked up the envelope, and – as one does when picking up any sacred object which has fallen – kissed it. He explained to the messenger,"This envelope was in the sanctified air of *Eretz Israel*, and it also has a degree of sanctity."

The Wood Merchant

A certain Jew who used to earn his living by selling logs of wood once came to Rabbi Avraham of Sochaczew, and asked the rabbi for help. It seemed that he had a contract to deliver a certain number of logs to the port of Danzig, by floating them down the Vistula. That year, due to a drought, the Vistula was too low to be of any use, and the man stood to lose a considerable amount of money for failing to fulfill his contract. When the man had finished making his request, Rabbi Avraham pushed him out the door, and exclaimed, "What do you want me to do? To supply water for the Vistula?"

Bitterly the man walked out. Before he had gone more than a few steps, Rabbi Avraham ran and told him, "If you donate a sizable amount of money to the settling of *Eretz Israel*, your logs will arrive in Danzig on time." The merchant immediately arranged for a considerable donation to the settling of *Eretz Israel*. Soon afterwards the Vistula started filling up, and the wood arrived in Danzig by the promised time.

Keeping Eretz Israel Alive

Rabbi Mordechai Yaffe made a point of remembering *Eretz Israel* and its poor. Each day he would pledge a sizable amount to the Holy Land. Throughout the day he gave money: on first getting up in the morning – even before beginning his daily prayers, before and after each meal, before and after his afternoon nap, and before and after each prayer service. In addition, he would donate money before and after every major or minor event in his life.

The Sound of the Shofar

Rabbi Shalom Ber, one of the leaders of the Lubavich Hasidic movement, once debated with the heads of the Hovevei Zion movement, who planned to move to *Eretz Israel*. "How do you have the nerve," he asked them, "to plan to move to *Eretz Israel* without first hearing that Elijah the Prophet, the harbinger of the redemption, has returned, and without hearing the *shofar* (ram's horn) which will signify the arrival of the Messiah?"

The members of Hovevei Zion replied, "We did hear the *shofar*, and whoever didn't hear it obviously didn't deserve to." Rabbi Shalom Ber understood the meaning of their answer, and a short time later asked the Chovevei Zion to take his son with them to *Eretz Israel*.

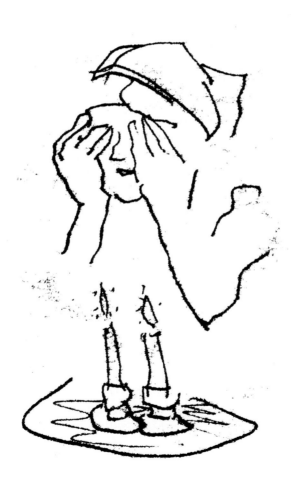

How to Preserve One's Money

Rabbi Nahman of Breslau once stated, "Whoever donates his money to the poor of *Eretz Israel* is assured that his assets will remain with him."

What Are We Doing?

On the first Sabbath after the Poles had raised their national flag in revolt in 1863, Rabbi Yitzhak Meir of Gur entered his *beth medrash* (study hall) to recite the *kiddush* ceremony over wine. As he prepared to begin reciting the text, he gave a deep sigh and said, "I am afraid that in the heavens there may be complaints against the Jews. We can all see how a nation such as the Poles is willing to sacrifice the lives of its sons in order to liberate the country from foreign rule, and what are we Jews doing to regain our freedom?"

Buying Eretz Israel

At one of his assemblies with his disciples, Rabbi Simha Bunim of Pzhysha wondered aloud why Moses Montefiore had not bought *Eretz Israel* from the Ottoman Empire, which owned it at the time. "But what will we do with it if he buys it?" asked one of the disciples. "After all, we have not yet been commanded by God to return to the country." "Don't say that," responded Rabbi Bunim. "If the land leaves the non-Jews' possession and comes into ours, God's redemption will have to follow soon afterward."

Contributing Money to Eretz Israel

Rabbi Moshe of Kobrin would normally expound at length on the holiday of Purim about *Eretz Israel*. It was the custom among his disciples that each would send *mishlo'ach manot*, the customary Purim gifts of food, by means of another who acted as his messenger. Each messenger would be paid for his services, and all the money which was earned was set aside for *Eretz Israel*. Rabbi Moshe used to say, "By contributing money to *Eretz Israel* we are fighting against our archenemy Haman, and this will bring about his downfall."

Living in Eretz Israel

A Personal Recollection

Dr. Eliezer Halevi was the personal secretary of Moses Montefiore when the latter visited *Eretz Israel*. In one of his letters, Dr. Halevi tells of Rabbi Dov Avraham of Abruch, who had settled in Safed in 1832:

"On Sabbath I was invited to be at the table of Rabbi Dov Avraham. That man is one of the greatest scholars I have met in my life. Not only does he serve without pay as the rabbi of the community, but he distributes whatever funds he has to the poor. From ten to fifteen people eat at his table each day. The fervor with which these people sang the *zemirot*, the traditional Sabbath songs, showed clearly that the melody truly came from the depths of their hearts."

Things Have Improved

When Rabbi Avraham Mordechai of Gur arrived in *Eretz Israel* and visited Jerusalem, Rabbi Avraham Yitzhak Hakohen Kook travelled to the outskirts of the city to welcome him. They shared the same car on their trip into the city.

Rabbi Avraham Mordechai began bemoaning the great decline in religious observance, and exclaimed, "Woe to us that we have lived to see the holy city of Jerusalem, which had previously been filled with sages and prophets, now filled with those who have rejected the commandments." Rabbi Avraham Yitzhak did not answer him, but rather changed the topic.

During their journey, they drove through the Valley of Hinnom (Gei Hinnom or Gehenna). "This place," said Rabbi Avraham Yitzhak to the Rabbi of Gur, "is Gei Hinnom. At the time of the prophets, Jews would sacrifice their children here to various idolatrous cults. In our times though, as you see, there isn't even a trace of such idolatry."

Honest Work

When Rabbi Velvele of Zbaraz moved to *Eretz Israel*, his wife preferred to become a washerwoman in order to support the family, rather than to live off charity. Once Rabbi Yaakov Shimshon of Sheptivka came for a visit. As he approached their home, he saw Rabbi Velvele's wife scrubbing the wash outside. Feeling how humiliating it must be for the wife of a prominent rabbi to have to do her wash in public, Rabbi Yaakov Shimshon was just about to leave so that he would not see the couple's humiliation.

At that moment, Rabbi Velvele's wife spotted him; she immediately felt his discomfort. "Do not be concerned, rabbi," she told him. "This is not my personal wash, but rather work that I undertake, and which ensures our liveli-

157

hood. Thank God that we are able to live in *Eretz Israel* and to live off our manual labor."

Rabbi Yaakov Shimshon entered their home and greeted Rabbi Velvele with great joy.

The Land is Exceedingly Good

Rabbi Aaron Moshe of Brody was one of the original disciples of the *Hozeh* (the "Seer") of Lublin. After he had settled in Hebron, his rabbi would appear to him in a dream and often clarify certain points in his Talmudic studies that were troubling him.

Once, a young man approached Rabbi Aaron Moshe and complained that even though he had already lived in *Eretz Israel* for a number of years, he still could not feel its sanctity or any stirring within himself to serve God in a better manner. Rabbi Aaron Moshe listened, but didn't answer a word.

That night the *Hozeh* appeared to Rabbi Aaron Moshe and told him, "In order for a person to be worthy of recognizing *Eretz Israel* as being 'exceedingly good,' as it is referred to in the Torah, he must first act in accordance with the saying of our Sages to be 'exceedingly humble.'"

It is said that Rabbi Aaron Moshe was one of the mourners of Zion, who mourned not only for the Divine Presence which had gone into exile with the Jews, but also for the Jews themselves who were still in exile.

Eventually Rabbi Aaron Moshe moved to Jerusalem, where he is buried. On his tombstone is carved, "A saintly, pure man who loved Jews."

When Does Eretz Israel Flourish?

When the Jews live in it, *Eretz Israel* is considered to be settled. If the Jews are exiled from it – even if other nations live there – it is considered to be a desert. It follows that only Jews can settle *Eretz Israel*.

Caring About Tomorrow

When the Kalisher Rabbi, Rabbi Haim Eliezer Waks, arrived in Jerusalem, he preached to the Jews residing there of the importance of engaging in agriculture, rather than relying on the *halukah* (charity collected throughout the world for distribution to the Jews in *Eretz Israel*). The Jerusalem Jews answered that farming provided an unsteady income, depending on each year's crops, while the *halukah* was at least steady. The rabbi then asked them, "What will you do if the *halukah* money suddenly stops?" "We are not worried about tomorrow," they replied. "Then," exclaimed the rabbi, "you are like the wicked person who says, 'Why should I be concerned about the tomorrow of the World to Come? I live only for today.'"

A *Sure Sign of Redemption*

Rabbi Mordechai Ashkenazi commented that the Talmud, in two separate passages, gives a clear indication that the most clear sign of the approach of the redemption is the sight of groves in *Eretz Israel* loaded with fruit. This is stated in Ezekiel (38:8), "But you, O mountains of Israel, shall shoot forth your branches, and yield your fruit to My people, Israel, for it (the redemption) is close at hand."

"*Jerusalem Didn't Like You*"

A certain Hasid moved from Poland to *Eretz Israel* and settled in Jerusalem. After having lived in the city for about a year, he decided that he was not able to adapt to the lifestyle in the town, and decided to return to his former home.

Before leaving Jerusalem, he went to his Rabbi, Rabbi Simha Bunim of Vorki, who lived in Jerusalem, in order to receive the rabbi's blessing for his forthcoming trip. While there, he explained to the rabbi at length the factors which had finally made him decide to leave the country.

The rabbi sighed a long sigh, from the depths of his heart, and told him, "I really pity you. Jerusalem evidently didn't like you. Had Jerusalem liked you, you would have liked Jerusalem."

A short time later the Hasid returned to Rabbi Simha Bunim to tell him that he had decided to stay after all.

Glossary

Important Note: The definitions given in this glossary pertain to the words as used in the context of this volume. Many words have additional meanings, but not as used here. For more detailed explanations, refer to any Jewish encyclopedia.

Aggadah: Parables, commentaries, legends, proverbs and stories, mainly derived from Biblical texts, expounding on their complexities and constituting one of the components of the Talmud and Midrash.

Ashkenazi (pl. *Ashkenazim*): A Jew whose ancestors originally lived in Germany or Poland.

Beit Midrash (literally "house of study"): An assembly hall used primarily for study of the sacred texts.

Dayan: Judge in a rabbinic court of law (the *Beth Din*), often the arbiter in disputes.

Din: Judgement, legal decision.

Eretz Israel (literally "land of Israel"): the Hebrew term for the territory later known as Palestine. The term dates back to Biblical times.

Galut (literally "exile"): The condition of the Jews living in foreign countries, without a land of their own and hence often subject to persecution and oppression. *"Galut"* implies the compulsory banishment of the Jews from the Land of Israel, in contrast to the term "Diaspora," which merely designates the dispersion of the Jews throughout the world in a more or less voluntary migration.

Halachah (literally "the way"): The Talmudic texts dealing with Jewish law. These texts normally are based on Biblical exegesis. By extension, the term now refers to the entire body of Jewish law, as it affects all aspects of Jewish life.

Hasid (pl. *Hasidim* – literally "pious"): A member of the sect founded approximately two hundred years ago by Rabbi Israel Baal Shem Tov (1700-1760) in Eastern Europe.

Heder: An old-style Jewish school for boys from post-infancy to about age thirteen, where they are taught Judaic studies exclusively (Bible, prayer, Mishnah, etc.)

Kabbalah: A body of works which interprets the sacred Judaic texts in a mystical fashion; a mystic trend in Judaism.

Mashal: A parable or fable; an allegorical story.

Midrash: A body of religious literature which strives to interpret the Biblical text, primarily in terms of the ethical and moral lessons to be deduced from the text. The bulk of this literature traces back to the first centuries C.E.

Minyan: The minimum quorum of ten males aged

thirteen or older needed for holding congregational services.

Mitnaged (pl. *Mitnagdim* – literally "adversary"): Those who opposed the Hasidic sect when it first appeared (and their spiritual descendants to this day), judging it to be revolutionary, dangerous and heretic.

Mitzvah (pl. *Mitzvot*): A commandment of the Torah, either positive or negative. Commandments are often classified, as, for example, those between man and his Maker, man and his fellow-man, commandments of the Holy Land, and those not dependent on being in any specific land.

Talmud: The collected records of the academic discussions on Jewish law by generations of scholars and jurists. There are two Talmuds: the Palestinian, compiled about 400 C.E., and the Babylonian, compiled about a century later.

Torah: Traditionally, the first five books of the Bible (the Pentateuch); in a more general sense, the word is used to refer to the entire body of Judaic law, both the written law given at Sinai and the commentaries on that law.

Tzaddik (literally "righteous one"): The title bestowed upon the head of any Hasidic sect.

Yeshiva: A Jewish traditional school, most often devoted almost exclusively to the study of the Talmud and other Judaic subjects.

Zohar (literally "splendor"): A Kabbalistic commentary on the Torah, traditionally attributed to Rabbi Shimon bar Yochai, who lived in the Talmudic era.

Bibliography

Hasidic Works

Bat Ayin: Oral discourses given each Sabbath and festival by Rabbi Avraham Dov Ber Avruch, Jerusalem, 1847.

Beit Aaron: Rabbi Aaron of Karlin, Piotrkov, 1910.

Butzina Denehora Hashalem: Collected writings of Rabbi Baruch of Medzibozh, Zitomir, 1865.

Degel Machaneh Efraim: Rabbi Moshe Haim Efraim of Sadylkov, 1883.

Derech Hasidim: Collected Hasidic writings arranged by topic (anonymous), Lemberg, 1876.

Dover Shalom: Collected discourses of Rabbi Shalom Rokach, Primishlan, 1910.

Geulat Ha'aretz: M. Ashkenazi, Warsaw, 1904.

Hassidic Anthology, The: Louis Newman, New York, 1963.

Igeret Hakodesh: Collection of discourses of Hasidic rabbis, Lwow, 1859.

Irin Kadishin: Discourses of Rabbi Yisrael of Rizhyn, Warsaw, 1895.

Kedushat Levi: Rabbi Levi Yitzhak of Berditchev, Warsaw, 1876.

Kehal Hasidim Hehadash: Lwow, 1902.

Keter Shem Tov: All the sayings of Rabbi Israel

Baal Shem Tov found in the sacred books of Rabbi Yaakov Yosef of Polnoye, Bnei Brak, 1957.

Kochavei Or: Stories of Rabbi Nahman of Breslau, gathered by Shmuel Halevi Horwitz, Jerusalem, 1933.

Likutei Moharan: Rabbi Nahman of Breslau, Jerusalem, 1874.

Likutei Ramal: Rabbi Moshe Leib of Sasov, Lwow, 1873.

Likutei Tefilot: Rabbi Nathan of Nemirov, Lwow, 1876.

Maaseh Tzaddikim: Stories about the Baal Shem Tov, Rabbi Baruch of Medzibozh, Rabbi Elimelech of Lizhensk, Rabbi Zusya of Hanipol, Rabbi Pinhas of Koretz, Lemberg, 1865.

Maasiyot Hagedolim Hehadash: Rabbi M. Soldovnik, Warsaw, 1925.

Maggid Devarav Leyaakov: Rabbi Dov Ber of Mezritch, Lemberg, 1897.

Midor Dor: M. Lipson, Tev Aviv, 1929.

Nahalah Leyisrael: Yisrael Zeev Horowitz, Jerusalem, 1882.

Noam Elimelech: Rabbi Elimelech of Lizhensk, Warsaw, 1881.

Nofet Tzufim: Rabbi Pinhas of Koretz, Warsaw, 1929.

Ohel Elimelech: Legends of Rabbi Elimelech of Lizhensk, Primishlan, 1914.

Pitgamin Kadishin Hashalem: Collection taken from the Baal Shem Tov, Rabbi Dov Ber of Mezritch, Rabbi Levi Yitzhak of Berditchev and other Hasidic rabbis, Lublin, 1889.

Pri Ha'aretz: Rabbi Menahem Mendel of Vitebsk, Jerusalem, 1954.

Ramatayim Tzofim: Explanation of the *Medrash Tanna D'bei Eliyahu*, based on sayings of the Hasidic masters, Warsaw, 1881.

Seder Hadorot Hehadash: Lemberg, 1865.

Sefer Hamidot: Rabbi Nahman of Breslau, Warsaw, 1912.

Shivhei Haran: Rabbi Nahman of Breslau with the account of his trip to Eretz Israel, Jerusalem, 1936.

Shivhei Tzaddikim: M. Tzitrin, Warsaw.

Sipurei Maasiyot: Rabbi Nahman of Breslau (S.A. Horodetsky), Berlin, 1922.

Siach Sarfei Kodesh (5 volumes): J.K.K. Rokotz, Lodz, 1929.

Tabur Ha'aretz: M. Kalirs, Tiberias, 1906.

Tiferet Banim: Warsaw, 1911.

Tiferet Hatzaddikim: G. Rosenthal, Piotrkov, 1928.

Tiferet Shlomo: Rabbi Shlomo of Radomsk, Warsaw, 1867.

Toldot Yaakov Yosef: Rabbi Yaakov Yosef of Polnoye, Warsaw, 1881.

Zichron Tzaddik: Rabbi S. Stam, Vilna, 1908.

Zimrat Ha'aretz: Rabbi Nahman of Breslau, Lemberg, 1876.

Collections and Sources for Hasidic Stories

M. Becker: *Parpera'ot Latorah* (Spices of the Torah), Jerusalem, 1980.

A. Ben-Yisrael: *Aggadot Ha'aretz* (Legends of Eretz Israel), Tel Aviv, 1925.

Y. Bernstein: *Mipi Rishonim Ve'aharonim* (From the Earlier and Later Sages), Jerusalem, 1980.

M. Buber: *Or Haganuz* (The Hidden Light), Jerusalem, 1969.

M. Cohen: *Al Hatorah* (On the Torah), Jerusalem, 1962.

B. Don, S. Raz: Eretz Hemdah (The Precious Land), Tel Aviv, 1971.

A. Frankel: *Yehidei Segulah* (The Select Individuals), Tev Aviv, 1969.

Heiman Hayerushalmi: *Nitzotzot Hage'ulah* (Sparks of the Redemption), Jerusalem, 1969.

S.A. Horodetsky: *Shivhei Habesht* (Praises of the Baal Shem Tov), Berlin, 1922.

Y. Kil: *Yisrael Uge'ulato* (Israel and its Redemption – a source collection) , Jerusalem, 1975.

Meyer Levin: *The Golden Mountain*, New York, 1932.

Y.L. Maimon (Fishman): *Midei Hodesh Behodsho* (Month by Month), Jerusalem, 1956.

A. Marcus: *Hahasidut* (Hasidism).

P. Sadeh: *Tikkun Halev* (Perfecting the Heart), Tel Aviv, 1981.

A. Steinman: *Kankan Hakesef* (The Silver Vessel – 4 volumes), Tel Aviv, 1970.

S. Zevin: *Sipurei Hasidim* (Hasidic Stories), Jerusalem, 1969.

Sources for Hasidic Legends of Eretz Israel

Y. Barnai: *Igrot Hasidim Mei'eretz Yisrael* (Hasidic Stories from Eretz Israel), Jerusalem, 1980.

Birkat Ha'aretz (Blessings of the Land), B.D. Kahana edition, Jerusalem, 1904.

Ginzei Nistarot (Hidden Treasures), C.A. Bochovsky edition, Jerusalem, 1924.

Hibat Ha'aretz (Love of the Land), B.D. Kahana edition, Jerusalem, 1897.

Y. Halperin, *Ha'aliyot Harishonot Shel Hahasidim Le'eretz Yisrael* (The First Hasidic Moves to Eretz Israel), Jerusalem, 1980.

A. Yaari, *Igrot Eretz Israel* (Letters of Eretz Israel), Ramat Gan, 1970.

General Works on Hasidism

Y. Alfasi, *Hahasidut – Pirkei Mechkar Vetoladah* (Hasidism – Chapters of Research and History), Tel Aviv, 1969.

Y. Alfasi, *Hahasidut Beromania* (Hasidism in Rumania), Tel Aviv, 1973.

Y. Alfasi, *Harav Mei'apta Ba'al "Ohev Yisrael"* (The Rabbi of Apta, Author of *Ohev Yisrael*), Tel Aviv, 1953.

Y. Alfasi, *Mechkerei Hasidut* (Studies in Hasidism), Tel Aviv, 1975.

Y. Alfasi, *Rabbi Nahman Mibratslav* (Rabbi Nahman of Breslau), Tel Aviv, 1953.

A. Avisar, *Sefer Hevron* (The Book of Hebron), Jerusalem, 1970.

A. Avisar, *Sefer Teveriya* (The Book of Tiberias), Jerusalem, 1973.

Y.S.Y. Hasida, *Hamishim Shaarei Hasidut* (Fifty Gates of Hasidism), Jerusalem, 1975.

S. Dubnow, *Toldot Hahasidut* (History of Hasidism), Tel Aviv, 1932.

S. Federbush (ed.), *Hahasidut Vetziyon* (Hasidism and Zion), New York, 1963.

Y. Greenstein, *Talmidei Habesht Be'eretz Yisrael* (Students of the Baal Shem Tov in Eretz Israel), Bnei Brak, 1982.

M. Gutman, *Torat Rabbi Pinchas Mikoretz* (The Torah Works of Rabbi Pinchas of Koretz), Tel Aviv, 1953.

S.A. Horodetsky, *Ali Tziyon* (Go Up to Zion), Jerusalem, 1940.

A. Kahana, *Sefer Hahasidut* (The Book of Hasidism), Warsaw, 1922.

Y.L. Maimon (Fishman), *Hatziyonut Hadatit Behitpatchuta* (Religious Zionism in its Development), Jerusalem, 1937.

M. Oriyon, *Ma'agalot Hahasidut* (The Circles of Hasidism), Jerusalem, 1978.

Z.M. Rabinowitz, *Hamaggid Mikoznitz* (The Maggid of Koznitz), Tel Aviv, 1947.

Y. Rafael, *Hahasidut Ve'eretz Yisrael* (Hasidism and Eretz Israel), Tel Aviv, 1940.

N. Shor, *Sefer Tzefat* (The Book of Safed), Tel Aviv, 1984.

Y.D. Wilhelm, *Dor Dor Ve'olav* (Each Generation and Its Movers [to Eretz Israel]), Jerusalem, 1946.

Articles on Hasidism

Y. Barnai, "Al Aliyato Shel Rabbi Avraham Gershon Mikitov Le'eretz Yisrael (On the Move of Rabbi Avraham Gershon of Kitov to Eretz Israel)," *Tziyon*, 42, 1977.

A. Ben-Yisrael, "Eretz Yisrael Besifrut Hahasidut (Eretz Israel in Hasidic Literature)," in *Sefer Hazikaron Le-A.Z. Rabinowitz*, Tel Aviv, 1922.

A.Y. Braver, "Lekorot Yishuv Hahasidim Be'eretz Yisrael (On the History of the Settlement of the Hasidim in Eretz Israel)," *Hator*, 16-17, 1924.

B.Z. Dinur, "Reishita Shel Hahasidut Visodoteha Hasotziali'im Vehameshihi'im (The Beginning of Hasidism and its Social and Messianic Principles)," in *Bemifne Hadorot*, Jerusalem,

1975.

S. Dubnow, "Hahasidim Harishonim Be'eretz Yisrael (The First Hasidim in Eretz Israel)," *Pardes*, 2.

A. J. Heschel, "Rabbi Avraham Gershon Kotover Ufarashat Aliyato Le'eretz Yisrael (Rabbi Avraham Gershon Kotover and His Move to Eretz Israel)," *HUCA*, XXXII, 1950-51.

S.A. Horodetsky, "Hahasidut Ve'eretz Yisrael (Hasidism and Eretz Israel)," *Hashaliach*, 8, 1901-02.

Mahanayim, Magazine of the Chaplaincy of the Israel Defense Forces, especially the articles by B. Landau and A. Yaari.

G. Scholem, "Mitzvah Haba'ah Be'aveira (A Good Deed Brought about by Committing a Sin)," *Knesset*, 2, 1937.

A. Schohat, "Shalosh Igrot al Eretz Yisrael (Three Letters on Eretz Israel)," *Shalem*, 1, 1975.

Y. Warfel, "Hahasidut Ve'eretz Yisrael Lehalachah Ulema'aseh (Hasidism and Eretz Israel in Theory and Practice)," *Sinai*, 1936.

Y. Weiss, "Reishit Tzemihata Shel Haderech Hahasidit (The Beginning of the Growth of the Hasidic Movement)," *Tziyon*, 16.